A POWERFUL ATTRACTION

DELANEY DIAMOND

Garden Avenue Press

A Powerful Attraction by Delaney Diamond

Copyright © 2018, Delaney Diamond

Garden Avenue Press

Atlanta, Georgia

ISBN: 978-1-940636-76-4 (Ebook edition)

ISBN: 978-1-940636-77-1 (Paperback edition)

www.delaneydiamond.com

"**A**ny questions?"

Alex Barraza, one of the owners at Newmark Advisors, looked around the conference room at the staff gathered for the usual end-of-week meeting. He stood with his legs shoulder-width apart, his broad-shouldered height dominating the room, and surveyed the group through a pair of silver-framed glasses. Several people shook their heads, but everyone remained silent.

"Okay, if there are no questions, let's get back to work."

Sherry Westbrook stood, grabbing her pen and notepad at the same time.

"Sherry, could you stay behind for a bit? I need to talk to you." Alex smiled briefly and then started erasing the charts and figures from the dry-erase board at the front of the room.

Sherry eased back into the chair as the rest of the staff filed out. Her gaze lingered on him, and she slowly took air into her lungs and shifted. She loved the way he said her name. He made it sound exotic with his rolled Rs and accented pronunciation, which never failed to make the hairs on the back of her neck stand at attention.

She really shouldn't have the hots for her boss, but Alex was the kind of man fantasies were made of. His wavy black hair glistened under the lights and curled against the collar of his dark jacket, while his solid-looking jaw, covered in a scruff of hair, screamed for a modeling contract. She'd been drooling over him since the first day she set foot through the door and he interviewed her.

Alex turned away from the board. "This won't take long." His voice was low, faintly accented because of his Colombian nationality, and smooth as silk. He resumed his position at the head of the conference table. "I know you're wondering why I asked you to remain behind, and it's for a very good reason. As I mentioned in the meeting, we signed a new client to the firm, Ovation Printing Company. The good news is, we have the business. The bad news is, they want us to conduct in-person meetings with their staff to assess their portfolios and offer advice."

"All thirty-five employees?" Sherry asked.

"That's correct."

"But why in-person meetings? We can do the assessments virtually."

"True, but the last investment firm they worked with didn't give the level of customer service they wanted, and that's why they decided to move their business."

He removed his glasses, setting them carefully on the table, and her stomach tangled into tighter knots at the better view of his face. His looks were why their female clients practically swooned at the sound of his voice and heaped hair-twirling, eyelash-batting adoration on him. Sherry had come close to doing the same on many occasions. She wished he didn't have such a nice mouth, with lips that were not too full or too thin, and hazel eyes whose light color was an attractive contrast to his dark hair and swarthy features.

Alex continued. "We want to show them why we're one of the fastest-growing investment firms in the country and make sure they understand we'll take good care of their personnel."

"That's a lot of meetings, which will take a lot of time," Sherry said.

Alex nodded. "That's why I've decided to have you work with me on this project. I want to make sure they're happy. Normally we'd do a simple rollover, but this time we're giving them the full treatment—analyzing each employee's current portfolio, conducting risk sensitivity, and recommending investment products."

"Why am I included on this project?" Sherry asked.

That was not a self-deprecating question. Alex was not only an owner, he managed some of the highest-performing portfolios in the company. He didn't need her. He could just as easily ask one of the admins to assist him.

"Because ever since you joined the staff two years ago, you've received the top customer service scores in the company," he replied. "With the two of us working together, I expect the transition to be a breeze."

Now she understood. Sherry considered customer service to be her strength. In an industry where seventy-five percent of the financial advisors were men, she differentiated herself by taking extra time to listen to her clients and establishing a rapport with them that put them at ease. She did her best work with the older crowd—seniors, widows—who could get confused by the unfamiliar terminology and overwhelmed by the figures and calculations. They were cautious and trusted her to take care of them, and she took great pride in doing so.

That Alex trusted her enough to pull her into the Ovation Printing Company project was huge. Unfortunately, that meant she'd be stuck working closely with him. A man whose very presence spiked her blood pressure and made her heart race out of control. This should be interesting.

"When do we start?" she asked.

"Monday. We'll meet in the small conference room at nine o'clock to review the transfer of information. We'll decide then how to divvy up the work, that kind of thing. Gina will be helping us with some of the paperwork. Any questions?"

"I can't think of any. But I'm sure I'll think of something later." Sherry gave a slight laugh.

He smiled, but hardly. When she first arrived, he used to smile more and had been more relaxed. Nowadays, he seemed more driven and less animated. He still smiled and was friendly, but the spark was gone.

"If you do end up thinking of a question later, feel free to reach out to me."

"I will."

"All right, that's it."

Sherry stood and gathered her belongings again and headed toward the door.

"And Sherry?" Alex called out to her.

Halfway across the room, Sherry turned to face him.

He rose from the chair to his imposing height, at least five or six inches taller than her. "I'll have Gina send over the rest of the details sometime this afternoon so you can review them before we get together on Monday."

"Oh." Sherry glanced at her watch. "I'm leaving work in a couple of hours to get ready for a full weekend. I have...big plans and, well, you don't want to hear about that..." Flustered at the intent way he'd started looking at her, she let the words trail off.

"Big plans? A...date?"

"Um, yes, actually."

Alex's eyes narrowed slightly, and an odd silence overtook the room. "New boyfriend?"

"Um, yes." His questioning made her uncomfortable and oddly, aroused at the same time.

He picked up his glasses but didn't put them on. He stared at them in his hands. "He's taking you to dinner, I suppose?"

"Yes. Dinner at my favorite restaurant and then a picnic on Saturday."

Alex put on his glasses. She couldn't read his expression, but his jaw had firmed and his eyes—they glinted with unexpressed emotion as the tension increased between them.

This wasn't the first time there'd been tension between them. It appeared from time to time. In Sherry's mind, it was from an unacknowledged attraction. Alex never touched her or made inappropriate remarks, but there were times when he looked at her in a certain way that made her wonder—did he feel it too? That surge of heat and longing that tormented her in his presence. Two years ago, within minutes of meeting and going through the interview process, that tension raised its ugly head, inexplicable and very present, like a shadowy specter between them.

"It's been what, a year since the last guy, hasn't it?"

Sherry blinked. "Yes, it has been," she replied, embarrassed and surprised he knew anything about the breakup from her cheating ex a little over a year ago.

How could he possibly know any detail about her love life? She didn't know anything about his, nor did anyone else on the staff, from what she could tell. No ring, so he was unmarried, and Sherry was close with his admin, Gina. She'd never divulged details about him sending flowers or other gifts to girlfriends. If he did, he took care of those tasks himself. There wasn't even a whisper of a woman in his life.

"Have fun," Alex said, though he didn't sound or look like he meant it. His face remained expressionless.

"Thank you. I will." Sherry turned around and hurried from the room.

⌘

ALEX WATCHED SHERRY FROM HIS OFFICE WINDOW AS SHE LEFT FOR the day. She glided down the cement steps in front of the building, turned left, and disappeared from view.

So, she had a new man. He was surprised it had taken so long. She was an attractive woman, with sensual brown eyes and a broad, slightly upturned nose. Her skin was a lovely shade of light brown and always glowed like she'd recently come in out of the sun.

He'd known from the beginning that she'd experienced the same tug of attraction he did, but he'd feigned indifference as best he could, transforming into a stoic statue every time she came near. Pretending that her close proximity didn't unnerve him, or that the scent of her perfume didn't release a primal need to grab and claim her.

The pencil in his hand snapped, and Alex looked down at the two pieces. Sighing, he tossed them into the trash can beside his desk and took a seat in his executive chair. He removed his glasses and pinched his nose.

What had he been thinking? Common sense dictated that he steer clear of her, but he was clearly a masochist, because he'd assigned her to work on this project with him. Working with her was a bad idea. He wanted her too much, and nothing should happen between them.

So what if his loins ached every time her round hips wiggled by him in one of those hip-hugging pencil skirts? So what if he'd fantasized dozens of times about all the ways he could fuck her?

Alex groaned and stroked his semi-erect penis through his pants. He'd never before been tempted to sleep with an employee, but Sherry Westbrook tested his resolve every weekday from eight in the morning to five in the evening.

"Forget her," he muttered.

There were valid reasons why they couldn't cross the line, the most obvious being that she worked for him. Now she was seeing someone else, and frustration at his inability to act tensed his shoulders and made him want to punch the wall.

But what could he do?

Not a damn thing.

❧ 2 ❧

"**H**oney, please be careful. There are all kinds of crazies out there and you don't know anything about this man."

Sherry rolled her eyes, listening to her mother's voice through the speakerphone as she prepared for her date. Excitement thrummed in her veins in anticipation of the night ahead, despite the conversation.

As usual, both of her parents were on the phone at the same time, being their usual protective selves. She spoke to them several times a week. Her mother tended to dominate the conversations, while her father went along with her shenanigans.

Leaning toward the mirror above the pedestal sink in her small bathroom, Sherry applied an extra layer of mascara to her left eye. "Mom, Dad, relax. I'm meeting him in a public place. What could possibly happen?"

She might have told a little lie to Alex. Stan wasn't her boyfriend, but she considered him a possibility. She'd met him online, but she'd done her due diligence. She had agreed to meet him at the restaurant instead of having him pick her up at her place, not to mention they'd talked numerous times over the past few months since he sent the first message to her inbox on Match.-

com. They graduated from the dating service's inbox, to exchanging emails, to exchanging phone numbers. He was funny, though a bit corny at times, but if he looked anything like his online photos, he was quite handsome.

Her mother sighed heavily. "I just want you to be careful, honey. Your last relationship ended when he broke your heart, but this man could be a serial killer."

Sherry shook her head and refused to respond to such an outrageous comment. She smoothed her hands over the knee-length black dress she wore. Sleeveless but fitted with an A-line skirt, the outfit made her look sexy without appearing as if she was trying too hard.

"Your mother's right. You have to be careful." Her father's voice filled the room. "Some of those men out there aren't good men. They're only looking for one thing, and you're better than that."

Sherry almost laughed. Her parents would have a stroke if they knew she was only looking for one thing too. She'd only been with two men in her life, and after talking to Stan for the past few months, she had gotten worked up with the anticipation of adding a third. While none of the conversations had delved too deeply into sex talk, they had played around with sexual innuendo and teasing banter that had re-sparked her libido.

She was definitely ready to do the nasty tonight. Since the breakup with her boyfriend, she'd almost sworn off men before realizing it was ridiculous to give up on them completely. She was only twenty-eight years old. A broken heart didn't last forever, and she did *not* want to give her ex the satisfaction of destroying her faith in love and romance.

She did realize, however, she hadn't been ready to start dating right after her relationship ended. So she took a break to concentrate on herself and work and spend time with her girlfriends. The break had paid off. She now felt emotionally ready to dive back into the dating pool, especially after several of her friends had found love in the past year.

"For a man, you have a very low opinion of men." Sherry checked to make sure there was no lipstick on her teeth.

"It's because I'm a man that I know," her father said.

"Duly noted, Dad. You guys, this conversation is going to have to come to an end." Sherry picked up her phone from atop the commode tank and turned out the light in the bathroom. The carpet in the bedroom muffled the sounds of her shoes as she walked to the bed and picked up her red clutch, which matched her red shoes. "I'm on my way to the restaurant."

"Call tomorrow and let us know how your date went," her mother said.

"Okay, Mom. I promise."

No point in arguing with them. Besides, Sherry knew she was lucky to have such loving parents. She was their only child, after they became pregnant late in life and were not able to get pregnant again. A miracle baby, they'd called her. Born so late that she fielded awkward conversations in high school when friends thought her parents were her grandparents.

She was not only loved, they would do anything for her. They paid for her education, and after she finished school and accepted a job in Atlanta, they took the journey with her, traveling over four hundred miles to help her get settled before returning to Kentucky.

She still remembered the trip to Walmart to buy supplies for her new apartment. And her parents had paid the first two months' rent and the deposit so she wouldn't have to worry about those expenses straining her bank account before she received a paycheck.

"Love you, honey," her mother said.

"Love you, too," her father interjected.

"Love you, guys. And don't worry about me, okay? I'll call you tomorrow."

The conversation ended, and Sherry sprayed perfume on the insides of her wrists and either side of her neck. If she were lucky tonight, she would not only be embarking on a brand-new relationship, she would get laid, too.

With a wicked laugh to herself, she tucked the clutch under an arm and left.

⚜

LA TAVOLA ITALIANO, ONE OF THE BEST RESTAURANTS IN TOWN, WAS understandably packed on Friday night. Seated at a two-top against the wall, Sherry checked the time on her phone again. Stan was late. Her stomach grumbled, a rebuke for not ordering at least some stuffed mushrooms—one of her favorite items on the menu —or a platter of bruschetta to hold her over.

She sipped water and then set the glass on the white tablecloth. She hadn't ordered a drink or even an appetizer because she'd wanted to wait until her date arrived. They'd agreed to meet at seven, but it was now seven thirty and there was no sign of him. Was he simply running late, or had he stood her up?

Surely he hadn't. They reconfirmed the date last night. He'd been excited—just as she had been.

She glanced at the phone on the table again. No text from him, and the one she sent ten minutes ago was still unanswered. Maybe he'd been in an accident, because this silence was unlike him.

Another twenty minutes passed and her stomach growled embarrassingly loudly. So loudly she hunkered down a little in the chair, hoping the people at the closest tables didn't hear. She should have eaten before coming out, but she'd expected Stan to be on time, and she'd wanted to save her appetite for her favorite restaurant.

Stan was now officially fifty minutes late, which meant he had stood her up. And she was *starving*.

The phone chirped beside her and she read the text.

Stan: Me and my ex have been talking for the past hour. We got back together. Sorry.

Wow.

Deflated, Sherry thought about the past three months of flirty texts and long conversations. And what about all the trouble she'd gone to just to get ready for tonight? She'd left work early to get her nails done, and her hair washed and styled into silky, shiny, loose curls that brushed her shoulders. She'd done a full face of makeup and even bought a new dress to impress him. All for naught.

Sherry channeled her anger and tapped out a quick message. *You're an ass.* She hit send. Then she turned her phone to silent and flipped it over onto its face. If he responded, she didn't want to know.

The waiter approached, a young Asian man with a sympathetic smile on his face. "Do you still need more time?" he asked.

She'd planned to leave, but Sherry felt guilty for holding his table for such a long time with only a glass of water. She could leave a nice tip, but why leave at all? Why waste a perfectly good outfit? And she was, after all, hungry. She would not let Stan force her back home. She'd had enough of letting a man's bad behavior dictate her actions.

She knew the menu inside out and chose to make the best of a bad situation. She was going to have dinner, dammit. By herself on a Friday night in a crowded restaurant.

"Actually, I don't need more time. The other person isn't going to make it."

"Oh."

She gave the waiter her order for a meal and a drink, and he left.

Idly, Sherry let her eyes wander around the room, and a bit of longing overcame her and her enthusiasm dimmed. Couples flirted across the tables from each other, and groups of friends laughed uproariously as they dived into the delicious-smelling Italian food served from the kitchen.

Maybe she should have tempered her excitement so disappointment didn't leave such a bitter aftertaste.

The waiter brought her drink, a Negroni, and set it on the table along with a platter of crisp bread and a small cart with different flavored olive oils and balsamic vinegar. "Your dinner order has been entered and should be up shortly."

"Thank you."

Sherry removed the orange peel from the side of the glass and sipped her cocktail.

"Don't tell me you got stood up."

On its own accord, her pulse bounced into alertness and then raced at the sound of the familiar voice.

Sherry looked up at Alex, standing beside her table, holding a tumbler with the remnants of a red drink in his hand. He wore the jacket from earlier in the day, but sans tie this time, with the top buttons of his shirt undone. He looked like he'd come straight from work to dinner.

"Excuse me?" Sherry said.

A sexy smirk lifted the corner of his mouth and caused tingling in the middle of her chest.

"I came in and sat at the bar behind you and saw you waiting for the past thirty minutes or so. Did your date have to cancel?"

Sherry considered lying, but what was the point? If Alex had been seated at the bar, then he'd accurately guessed she'd been waiting for her date, until a few minutes ago when she finally placed an order.

"Yes, he had to cancel," she admitted reluctantly.

"That's too bad." His face gave nothing away. "Then you shouldn't mind some company."

"That's mighty presumptuous of you," Sherry said.

"Am I wrong?"

Sherry shrugged. "It's a free country. You can have a seat anywhere you like." She spoke in a dismissive voice, though she would welcome the company.

"That doesn't answer my question."

They stared at each other.

"No, you're not wrong," Sherry admitted. "You're welcome to join me."

Alex sat down, and she made a conscious effort to tamp down

the excitement that shot through her arteries. He signaled for the waiter.

The young man hurried over. "Yes, sir."

"I'll have another Americano, please."

"Anything to eat?"

He paused and looked across the table at Sherry. "I'll have whatever she's having."

"You don't know what I'm having. You might not like it," Sherry said.

"You said this is your favorite restaurant, so I'm going to assume that's because the food is excellent. I'm also going to assume you made a good decision and I'll enjoy whatever you ordered."

"That's very trusting of you."

"I have good instincts," he said smoothly.

The waiter glanced knowingly between the two of them, the corners of his mouth tilting upward. He scribbled on his notepad. "Be right back."

"So, your hot new man stood you up. What's the name of this horrible person?" Alex asked.

"His name is Stan, and this was our first date," Sherry said.

"Ahh, so he's not your boyfriend?"

Sherry grimaced, kicking herself for accidentally contradicting what she'd told him at work.

"He's not my boyfriend per se, but we've been talking for the past few months. I thought I knew him well, but..." She shrugged. "He got back together with his ex." She picked at the white tablecloth. At least Stan didn't turn out to be a serial killer.

"Word of advice," Alex said, lowering his voice. "Never trust a man named Stan. Every Stan I know is a person of poor character."

She laughed. "What? That's not true."

"No, it's not. But it made you smile."

Oh. Sherry didn't know how to reply to that statement.

Alex's gaze swept over her. "You look lovely tonight."

"Better than at work?"

"You were lovely at work, too, but yes—this is better."

"You're not supposed to say that!"

She couldn't blame him for the remark because she did look fantastic in her black dress and red shoes. Her hair looked great, and the red lipstick made her full lips appear even more prominent.

"Would you prefer that I lie to you?"

"No, actually." Sherry sipped her drink and eyed him over the rim. "And what are you doing here?"

"Would you believe I was stood up, too?"

"No way." A twinge of jealousy twisted in her stomach.

He nodded. "By Rashad." Rashad was his best friend and the co-owner of Newmark Advisors.

"Oh." The jealousy dispersed, replaced by happy relief. She pressed her lips together so she wouldn't smile.

"We were supposed to meet for drinks and dinner, but like you, he stood me up for a woman."

"I'm sorry to hear that."

He shrugged. "I guess we have to keep each other company, yes?" His gaze skimmed over her, prickling the skin of her bare arms.

"I guess so." The night might have just gotten interesting.

🦋 3 🦋

Three hours.

For three hours he'd sat and talked to Sherry until the restaurant was almost empty. Only one other table remained occupied. Six people sat in a booth at the back of the dining room, and laughter erupted from them every now and again.

He and Sherry had covered every topic imaginable, including work, hobbies, relationships, and family. He learned that she was an only child and shared that he was raised by his grandfather, who'd passed away when he was twelve. After that, he was shuffled from home to home until he traveled from Colombia to the United States to attend school at eighteen. She talked about her volunteer work and how she'd lived in Atlanta for almost six years but didn't know the city as well as she'd like, while he made a point of exploring in his free time—jogging at various parks in the metro area, or lounging at coffee shops—all of which had served him well in drumming up new clients.

He'd enjoyed every minute spent in her company, time slipping by unnoticed while they idled over lasagna and a robust Brunello wine. Everything was delicious, but the meal paled in comparison to the woman who sat across from him.

"So you think trust is the most important part of a relationship?" Alex asked, continuing their conversation.

Normally, getting into such a deep discussion would make him retreat, but not so with Sherry, who shared her innermost thoughts in an open, honest way. And then there was her beauty —which shone from the inside out. She was obviously sweet-natured despite the attempt to project a cool, unaffected exterior at work.

The urge to get closer had only increased as each hour ticked by. He ached to see every inch of her skin. He wanted to taste her sweetness, and he'd start with licking from her cleavage, up her smooth throat, and then sucking that plump lower lip into his mouth.

"Trust is really important, no doubt." Sherry paused, her forefinger and thumb loosely trailing up and down the stem of her half-filled wine glass. "Trusting my family, my friends, my lover. Without trust, a relationship is fractured, don't you think?"

Alex nodded, staying silent because he knew she had more to say.

"I'm a little adamant about trust because of my last relationship. My ex, upwardly mobile man that he is, was sneaking around my back with a local socialite. He has aspirations to go into politics one day, so her family connections come in handy. I learned all of this at the same time I found out his business trips turned out to be trips to her family's homes in the Caribbean and Europe. Eighteen months down the drain."

"*Hijueputa.*"

"Yes—to whatever that means."

"It's not a nice word. It's the way we say 'son of a bitch' in Colombia. How did you find out about the other woman?"

She heaved a sigh. "A friend saw a photo of them in the paper, at a charity event at the Hilton. She told me about it, and I confronted him. He didn't bother to deny he had cheated on me with her. He seemed relieved, to be honest. The lying must have been taking a toll on his conscience."

Alex frowned. "You sound sympathetic."

"Oh no, I'm not." She shook her head vigorously, and her voluminous curls bounced on her head. "I still think he's a horrible person, but that doesn't mean he didn't feel guilty about what he did. At least, that's the way I perceived his reaction. Anyway, as you pointed out earlier today, I took almost a year to jump back into dating." His heart clenched at the sadness in her eyes.

"Then, when you jump back into dating, you get stood up by a man who goes back to his ex-girlfriend."

"Just my luck." A pained smiled this time. "What's most important to you in a relationship?" Sherry asked.

Alex thought for a moment. "Love."

"Love?" Both eyebrows rose.

"Yes. When you love someone, everything else falls into place. Respect, protection, consideration of the other person's feelings— all naturally occur when your love is genuine. I suppose because I never had that growing up, unconditional love is important and absolute to me." He'd never shared his thoughts on love with anyone else, nor had he ever admitted how much he craved it because it had been missing from his childhood.

Sherry pursed her lips. "My parents have that kind of love. They're lucky."

"Not lucky. Successful relationships involve hard work and commitment. You have to want success, and put in the work. It's like anything else."

Sherry nodded, then glanced around the restaurant and straightened suddenly, as if realizing for the first time that most of the patrons were gone. "We should probably leave."

Behind the bar, the bartender was packing up glasses, and a couple of servers sat at a table rolling silverware and napkins for the next day. The patrons from the back booth sauntered in a line toward the front door.

"You're right. Otherwise, they might kick us out."

She nodded and reached for her purse.

"Dinner's on me," Alex said, fishing out his wallet.

"Absolutely not."

"And why not?"

"Because it's inappropriate."

"Why?"

"Because you shouldn't be saddled with my meal, Alex."

"I invited myself to join you, remember? And I don't mind."

"Let me pay for my own dinner."

"No."

"The tip, then?"

"*No*. If it makes you feel better, consider this a business dinner. I'll add it to my expense report. After all, we did spend some talking about work." He called over the waiter, who approached and placed the bill on the table. Alex perused the items. Satisfied, he handed over the card with the bill.

Sherry bit the bottom corner of her lip, holding the scarlet-tinged flesh hostage between her teeth—which he longed to do himself. "You really don't have to do this."

"I'm not going to keep arguing with you, Sherry."

"Fine. I won't argue, but since you bought dinner, the least I can do is buy dessert."

"Dessert?" Alex looked around at the empty restaurant. "It's a bit late for that, isn't it?"

"Not really. There are places still open. We can go somewhere and listen to music and have dessert." She spoke with a certain amount of hesitation. "Unless you have a curfew…?"

Alex laughed softly. "No, I don't have a curfew."

"Then dessert is on me."

He studied her for a moment. She obviously wanted to spend more time with him, and he wanted to spend more time with her, but it wasn't a good idea. He couldn't risk getting involved with Sherry, and the burden of resisting the temptation she presented ate at him.

"I'll have to pass."

"Are you turning me down?" she asked with a little laugh.

"It's late," he said, by way of explanation.

"Late. Oh. So you do have a curfew, or maybe someone waiting at home for you?"

"I don't have anyone waiting at home for me," he said quietly.

"I see."

Her lips firmed, and he knew right away that he'd upset her. All the progress they'd made in the past few hours disappeared. Shit.

"Sherry—"

"No, it's fine. Believe me." She tucked her phone into her purse.

"Sherry." He covered her hand, and when she tried to withdraw, he tightened his hold. All night he'd fought the urge to touch her. Just reach across the table and hold her hand or press her palm to his mouth. Now that he had, his insides tightened with the enormity of the moment. And how much he wanted this woman—needed her on a level he couldn't comprehend. "This isn't a rejection of you."

"You must have misunderstood, Alex. There was nothing on offer except music and dessert. You have to go home, fine. As far as I'm concerned, the night is still young, and I'm going to enjoy myself, by myself." She pulled away her hand.

His fist tightened on the table. "What does that mean?"

She didn't get to answer because the waiter brought back the credit card receipt right then.

"Thank you for joining us for dinner this evening. Good night to both of you." The young man left.

Sherry stood abruptly from the table, and Alex swiftly signed the receipt and followed after her, admiring her graceful, angry movements in a pair of stilettos that showed off gorgeous legs covered in black silk stockings.

The manager stood at the door and bade them a good night before letting them out and locking the door behind them.

"Which one is yours?" Alex asked.

"I didn't drive. I'll just call a cab."

"I can give you a ride. I'm in the Porsche." He angled his chin toward the black vehicle in the middle of the mostly empty lot.

She turned away from him. "No, thanks. I'll be fine. I found my way here. I'll find my way to the next destination."

"Where are you going?"

In short order, he'd become territorial, wanting to keep her to himself. The way she was dressed, she would have no problem getting attention from any number of men, and the thought of her giving her digits to one of them and embarking on a new relationship damn near gave him an ulcer.

"Don't worry about it," she said.

"What the hell is your problem?" Alex snapped.

She turned on him with wide eyes. "What the hell is yours? You turned me down, and now you want to find out my itinerary? Whatever I decide to do after I leave here is my business, just like whatever you decide to do after you leave is your business. I only wanted us to go somewhere and have dessert and listen to music. I enjoyed your company and wanted to spend more time talking to you. That's it."

"That's it? That's all you wanted?"

"What else is there?"

"Don't pretend with me."

"I'm not pretending! Whatever you think I—"

He laughed softly, bitterly. Maybe they'd spent too much time together. Maybe he'd had too much to drink. But a sudden recklessness invaded his thoughts, and words that he would never think to say otherwise spilled from his mouth.

"You're terrible at pretending, you know that?" Every bit of banked frustration that had accumulated over the past couple of years beat down on him with relentless force. "Every day I look into those pretty brown eyes, and I see how much you want me. And you have no goddamn idea how hard it is to resist you."

Her lips parted, as if she were about to say something, and then she swallowed. "I...I don't—"

"Don't deny it," Alex growled. "Don't you fucking deny it. We both know that cake and ice cream wasn't the only thing on offer tonight. I can't stop thinking about fucking you, and if you think about it even half as much as I do, that's pretty damn frequent."

Sherry seemed at a loss for words. Hell, he was at a loss for words. He hadn't anticipated admitting any of that when he started talking. Maybe he *had* drunk too much. Or maybe he was tired of fighting these feelings that tortured him day after day, his break coming—minor though it was—when he left the office and didn't have to see her until the next morning.

"Okay, you want the truth." Her voice trembled, and she tilted her chin higher, looking boldly into his eyes. "I admit it. I want you too. I want to screw your brains out, and it makes me testy and edgy all day, every day. And I have to remind myself to be nice to my customers and polite to my coworkers because it isn't their fault that I find you attractive and wish that, just once, you would give a clear signal that you feel the same. Satisfied? So now what, Alex? I'm about to crawl out of my skin, and we've both admitted what we feel, but the ball's in your court now. What are you going to do about it?"

❧ 4 ❧

She must be out of her mind, but after laying bare her secret desires, Sherry remained frozen, in a limbo state that left her holding her breath for Alex's response.

He ran his fingers through his hair and gazed into the distance. Not a word. Not a single word.

He didn't want her. At least, not enough to act on his feelings. Disappointment turned sour in her stomach. She'd thrown herself at him and...nothing.

"Obviously you're not interested, so I'll find someone else to lavish my attention on." Sherry swung away from him, not sure what to do next, but certain she needed to get as far away from Alex as she could.

A strong hand encircled her wrist and swung her back around. Sherry gasped, as Alex hauled her into his chest, knocking the wind from her lungs and the purse from her hands. He shoved his fingers into her hair, cupping the back of her head and securing her in place.

He brought his face so close to hers that his breath feathered across her lips. "Your attention belongs to me," he ground out.

They were smashed against each other—chest to chest, thigh to thigh.

His gaze dipped to her lips, and she inhaled in anticipation, ached with the need to feel his mouth pressed to hers in the same way other parts of their bodies were pressed against each other.

Alex muttered in Spanish and then crushed his mouth to hers. The force of the kiss scattered all thought and Sherry moaned. At last! She wrapped her arms around his torso as his firm mouth traveled over hers with intensity. He plucked at her lower lip and traced his tongue along the fullness of its edge. With shaky, shallow breaths, she kissed him back with the same ardor and silently pleaded for more, curling her fingers into the fine material of his jacket and whimpering when he cupped her bottom with one hand and squeezed.

He guided them back to the building, away from the brilliant lights and into a dim corner. The hand at the back of her head lowered to her nape, and he used his thumb at the edge of her jaw to tilt back her head.

He kissed and sucked on her neck with the same passion and unrestrained dedication he did her mouth. Her sex throbbed and her panties grew wet at the unrelenting seduction of his mouth. She was damn near dizzy with lust.

Sherry let out a small cry as he edged below her collarbone to her ample cleavage. Grabbing a fistful of his soft hair, she thrust her aching breasts in an open invitation to his mouth.

But he didn't give her what she wanted. Instead, his lips climbed back up to suck on her neck. Sherry whispered her discontent with unintelligible words meant to prod him lower so he could take one of her aching nipples in his mouth. Her fingers tightened in his hair and she wrapped an arm around his neck as his warm breath and hungry, open-mouthed kisses beat against her skin.

"Your place or mine?" he asked in a husky voice, close to her ear.

"Mine."

"Where?"

She gave him the address.

"Too far. There's a Winthrop Hotel a couple blocks down. We'll go there."

"Okay," she said with breathless anticipation. She never for a second considered refusing. Finally, after years of yearning, she would spend the night with Alex.

He lifted his head and looked into her eyes. Grabbing her ass again, he forced her into contact with the hardness in his pants. He kissed once more, mouth brutal, almost savage in the way he sealed the bargain they'd just made.

"Let's go." Alex took her hand, and they picked up her purse on the march to his sports car.

Sherry settled on the seat and watched him walk around the hood to the driver side. Her body was on fire, and she felt as if she would jump out of her skin.

They took off from the parking lot, and during the short drive, neither of them said a word. The thickness in the air promised sex, and she feared that if she said a word she'd spoil the mood and Alex would change his mind.

But glancing at him from the corner of her eye, all she saw was a determined man, eyes focused on the road ahead.

❃❃❃

SHERRY DIDN'T HAVE TIME TO PAY ATTENTION TO THE EXQUISITE ROOM at the Winthrop Hotel. She only had eyes for the man before her—a man who made her want to behave out of the ordinary. To do things she wouldn't normally do—like go to a hotel with her boss and have him make love to her.

Alex tossed his jacket and shirt onto an armchair. Holding her hand, he backed up toward the bed and sat down, pulling her on top of his lap so she straddled his thighs. The pounding ache in her groin increased as he smoothed his hands up her thighs beneath the dress. His touch eased from her knees up to the edge of her panties. She squeezed her butt cheeks together, breath hitching at the slow but sensual touch.

Even in the dim room, Sherry could make out the near perfection of his form—his nose, the rigid set of his hair-rough jaw, the curve of his soft lips, and the powerful muscles beneath the smooth skin of his shoulders and arms.

Taking his time, he kissed her neck and moved the strap of the black dress down her arm so he could press his lips to her shoulder as well.

Sighing, Sherry arched her throat into his mouth and moaned when he thrust his pelvis upward, teasing her with the promise of the hardness between his thighs. She could almost come from that pressure alone.

Breathing heavily, she rose onto her knees and kissed him with a slow, sweet, lingering caress. He was such a good kisser, lips so soft and moist she could almost spend all night with the mouth-to-mouth contact. Yet that wouldn't be enough, because the pounding ache in her loins had to be assuaged. Eagerly, she plied kisses along his strong throat, eliciting a groan of satisfaction from deep in his chest.

Alex stood and set her on the carpet, and their clothes slipped away in a fog of desire. One minute Sherry was standing before him fully dressed, the next she was naked on her back on the plush white duvet, his lips to her bosom. Their hands roamed freely, exploring the terrain of each other's bodies. He licked from her breasts up to her throat. He licked as if he'd been waiting to do it all night, groaning as if the taste of her skin was the best thing he'd ever had.

He concentrated on her swollen nipples, and the curl of his pink tongue against the burnt-caramel tips had to be the most erotic sight she'd ever seen. Her fingers climbed into his hair and urged him to continue the attack on her senses. Raking her nails down his back, she reveled in the ripple of muscles under his skin.

Settled between her spread thighs, Alex kissed her softly, gently, as if it were the first time. Winding her arms around his neck, Sherry opened her mouth to his tongue and deepened the contact, creating a greater sense of urgency between them. She arched restlessly, undulating her hips against his pelvis and the hard pulse of his arousal trapped between them.

Rolling onto his back, Alex took Sherry with him. He caressed her back, buttocks, and thighs, and she whimpered softly, sliding her leg along his and sinking her teeth into his left bicep.

Their lovemaking was slow and leisurely as they explored each other. Sherry had fantasized about him for so long that she wanted to take her time getting acquainted with every bit of his beautiful body. She tongued his nipples, and the flat disks turned hard. She showered his broad chest with attention—kissing and caressing the surface from left to right, down to the trail of hairs that led to between his thighs.

Alex eased her onto her back, and she again rubbed her smooth thighs against his hairy legs. The contrast in texture was unbearably erotic. She gently sucked on the side of his neck and tasted his skin before nipping at his collarbone.

He spread his knees and pried her legs apart.

"Alex," she moaned.

"*Sí, amor.*"

He knew. The need had become so great that she couldn't articulate what she wanted him to do. She had become a mindless fragment of her former self, focused only on the pleasure he imparted with each touch. But he understood.

Alex retrieved a condom and then rejoined her on the bed. Sherry opened her arms in welcome, eager to feel the weight of him again. He drove up into her, the juices coating her canal allowing him to enter with ease. He buried his hot, thick flesh inside, his deep stroking making her moan his name.

Her mind unraveled under the sheer force of the pleasure he inflicted.

"*Dios,*" Alex said. He let out a groan that could only be described as tortured. "You feel so much better than I ever expected."

"Alex," she whispered, clinging to him. Forehead to forehead, they moved in sync. Needing him deeper, Sherry dug her nails into his sides and closed her eyes, letting the delicious sensation that traveled over her skin engulf her.

He sank into her, over and over again, his breath turning choppy as he struggled to maintain restraint while delivering the utmost pleasure.

"Yes. Like that." Sherry sucked air between her teeth, certain this slow, exquisite torture would be the death of her.

Alex lifted her leg over one arm, and with the position change, he switched up his slow thrusts into rapid, hard drives. The shocking tempo change made her cry out. Then she met each powerful motion with rapid responses of her own, her exploring fingers climbing back into his hair. Faster and faster he went, his mouth moving to her tender throat and kissing the sensitive spot right below her chin.

Sherry bucked beneath him, gasping for air, breathing choppy as his body owned hers.

He didn't stop until her inner walls clenched around him and she called out his name. A wave of ecstasy engulfed her, and only then did he claim his own release.

৺ 5 ৈ

S herry squinted, slightly disoriented at the light pouring through the big windows that took up half the wall. She wasn't at home. Then she remembered that she and Alex had spent the night together. First talking over dinner and then arguing in the parking lot before coming to the hotel and making love twice.

She heard muffled movements and rolled onto her side. Light came from under the bathroom door, which was where Alex must be.

She burrowed deeper under the thick duvet and soft sheets, pointing her toes and stretching her legs. She turned her nose into the pillow, which smelled like him and made her curl the same toes at the memory of their intense lovemaking.

His thoroughness had made her believe that he knew her body better than she did. She didn't regret not one kiss, caress, nor one part of the night she spent in his arms, but what now?

Parts of her still ached for his touch. Her nipples swelled and she moaned quietly. Even the soft linens proved to be too much for the sensitive peaks, and she touched them gingerly, wishing his hands were on her body instead.

Alex exited the bathroom, fully dressed in the clothes he'd worn last night. When he saw her awake, he paused in the middle of the floor.

Holding the sheet over her nakedness, Sherry sat up and smoothed a hand over her disheveled hair. "You're leaving? No breakfast?" She wanted—no, needed—to extend their time together.

He shook his head regretfully. "I have to run. I'm going to see a friend in the hospital, and I need to go home and change before I head over there. I can't get out of it."

"I wouldn't expect you to."

He studied her for a bit, his emotions veiled behind a neutral expression.

"You look like you want to say something," Sherry remarked.

"I do, but I don't want it to sound terrible." He took a deep breath. "Last night... What happened between us can't happen again."

A shaft of pain sliced across her chest. Sherry swallowed. "I see."

"It's for the best. For both of us." He didn't move, but the huskiness of his voice and the smoldering heat in his eyes betrayed the lies his lips told.

"I'm not arguing."

"It's just that you work for me, and...and I—" He swallowed back whatever he'd been about to say. It seemed he was trying to convince himself as much as her. "It could never work because you work for me and people would talk."

Be bold. Be daring for once in your life. "We don't have to tell anyone. It could be our secret," Sherry said softly.

Alex swore under his breath and ran his fingers through his rumpled hair, causing it to fall across his forehead in the most adorable, haphazard waves. "No," he said firmly, more to himself than to her. "I can't. I really regret this, but it's for the best."

Her gaze dropped to the erection tenting his trousers. "Are you sure?"

A long pause filled the room. Then he swore again, louder this time, and in two long strides was at the bed. He grabbed her and caught her lips with his. They tumbled back onto the sheets, him on top of her.

She reached between them and stroked his erection, tearing a groan from the depths of his chest. He pushed away the sheet and fastened his lips on her nipples.

"Yes," Sherry breathed, spreading her arms wide and arching her back as she indulged in the suction of his mouth.

"This is the last time." Alex kissed his way down the middle of her stomach.

Her belly quivered as his tongue swirled around her navel. Sliding a hand between her legs, he cupped her sex as if he owned it. Then he dragged his tongue across her slit, groaning as he indulged in the sticky wetness.

"Sweet," he whispered.

Sherry shoved her fingers into his hair, twisting against the teasing caress. "Alex," she gasped.

He pushed her onto her stomach. His hand smoothed down the curve of her bottom and nudged her legs apart. Sherry closed her eyes tight and lifted her bottom, ready for whatever he intended to do to her.

Soon he was naked from the waist down and inside her.

"We can't do this again," he muttered beside her ear.

"Never again. Last time," she panted, gripping the thick duvet and knowing full well if he approached her in the future, she would say yes without hesitation.

"Dammit, you feel incredible." He held on to her hips as he pushed in deeper.

Sherry moaned into the soft linens, lifting her ass into each thrust.

They were not making love like last night. He fucked her, good and hard, as if he needed it—and so did she.

No way this could be the last time. Because she was certain she could never, ever have enough of this man. And if this was a mistake, it was the best mistake she'd made in a long time.

❧ 6 ❧

He'd screwed up, but rectifying the situation was an easy fix.

Alex climbed out of his Porsche and ignored the admiring glances he received from a couple of women who'd just exited the elevator in the parking garage. Briefcase in hand, he jogged down the stairs to street level and walked briskly toward the office building where he worked.

On Sunday, he'd had clarity of thought. He would simply remove Sherry from the Ovation Printing project. It was that simple. Then they'd go back to business as usual. *No problema.*

Yet when he reached his office, his resolve almost crumbled at the sight of Sherry bent over his secretary's shoulder, looking at the computer screen.

She wore her hair bone-straight today, parted in the middle. From his vantage point, he saw down her silk blouse to the fullness of her breasts. His mouth watered in memory at the pleasure he'd taken in sucking the nipples.

Both women looked up. "Good morning," they said in unison.

Gina, his secretary, coupled the greeting with a wide smile. Efficient and friendly, she wore her hair in a thick Afro that framed her face. Sherry, however, returned her attention to the computer almost immediately.

"Good morning," Alex said. He marched to the door, thinking he should take a moment to regroup before calling Sherry into a meeting, but changed his mind at the last minute. His gaze slid to her backside in the horizontally striped pencil skirt as she remained bent over Gina's desk. "Sherry, may I see you in my office, please?"

She straightened. "Now?"

"Yes, now."

"I'll show you how to do part two when I get finished," she said to Gina.

"Thank you," Gina said.

Alex entered the office and walked behind his desk, putting as much distance between him and Sherry and possible. He placed his briefcase flat on top of the neat surface and turned on the TV secured to the wall. It remained on mute, displaying the latest in stock market news. He waited as Sherry closed the door and came forward. She clasped her hands together in front of her.

"I've had some time to think about this weekend," he began. He fiddled with papers on his desk. The urge to pull her close and press her soft body into his was too strong. "Of course I realize I complicated the situation with that last...episode, for lack of a better word. But what I initially said still holds true. We can't cross the line again, and my concern is that because of what happened, working together will be a problem. Therefore, I've decided to remove you from the Ovation project. I think it's best for both of us." The silence in the room made him look up. Sherry's lips were pressed together in a tight line.

"So you're removing me because we had sex?" she asked.

"No." That was exactly what he was doing.

"Are you sure? You've barely looked me in the eye since I walked in. I won't tell anyone what we did. I won't jeopardize your precious reputation."

She appeared upset, which was not his intention. He was

giving her a way out. Giving them both a way out of what would certainly be an uncomfortable work environment.

"I don't care about *my* reputation. If anyone's reputation would be tarnished, it's yours."

"I'm a big girl, and I can take care of myself. We agreed that what happened between us would never happen again. Why remove me from the project?"

He silently assessed her, the way she seemed emboldened, speaking in firmer tones. He'd never heard her speak in that tone before.

"We're not animals who lack control. Surely we can keep our hands to ourselves and respect each other's boundaries."

Speak for yourself, Alex thought.

"There's a lot of work to be done, and I want to help. This is the kind of thing I like to sink my teeth into," Sherry continued.

The same way she'd sunk her teeth into his flesh.

"All right, if you're sure and this is what you want to do. We can continue to work together if it doesn't make you uncomfortable." Alex snapped open his briefcase.

"Working with you doesn't make me uncomfortable, Alex."

His gaze flew to hers. She'd said his name in the same soft, breathy voice she'd used when they'd made love. Gooseflesh rose on his skin as he remembered all the ways she'd said his name.

Yes, Alex, yes.

Please, Alex.

Oh god, Alex.

He sat in the chair to hide the erection that started rearing its head. "All right. We finish the project and keep our hands to ourselves." He hoped he wouldn't regret this decision.

"Thank you."

She spun around and walked toward the door. His gaze dropped to her round bottom, which had more than adequately cushioned his thrusts. He'd tasted every inch of her, so it was impossible to forget anything they did. Impossible to forget how tight and wet she'd been, or the perfection of her caramel-tipped breasts. How was he supposed to get any work done with those memories stamped in his brain?

He was doomed.

◌❀◌

SHERRY DROPPED A STACK OF PRINTOUTS ONTO ALEX'S DESK. HE wasn't in the office at the moment, thank goodness.

The last four days had been torture, but she'd brought it on herself. She stayed in a constant state of arousal, which made it hard as hell to concentrate. She shouldn't have insisted on staying on the project. She still wasn't sure why she did when Alex had given her a way out of the torment of working with him for hours on end in his office. It was one of the biggest offices in the company, but way too small for the tension that constantly hovered between them.

"Is that everything?" Gina asked, walking up beside her.

Sherry nodded and tapped the pages. "Yep, and just in time for lunch." She laughed. "Everyone completed the risk assessment modules, and all the analyses are done. Monday we can start setting up meetings to offer advice on products for each employee's portfolio."

"That's great. You guys are moving really fast on this," Gina said.

"Yeah, we are, aren't we?"

Sherry didn't doubt for one second that Alex wanted to complete the Ovation project as quickly as she did. The sexual tension that had always existed between them had only intensified. Two nights this week they had worked late, poring over the data, each at opposite ends of the office so as not to get too close.

Gina propped one hand on her hip. "So, we never got to talk about your date last Friday night. I know you've been busy, and I've been trying to be polite and not be too nosy. But I can't wait for you to broach the topic anymore. What happened with Stan?"

Gina had encouraged Sherry to try online dating. She'd had

successful relationships over the years and had recently gotten engaged to a man she met online.

"He stood me up." Sherry grimaced.

"Oh no! That jerk. Have you heard from him since?"

"Not since Friday night, when he texted to say he was getting back together with his ex-girlfriend."

Gina groaned and sympathetically rubbed a hand up and down Sherry's arm. "I'm so sorry, girl. I hope you don't give up on online dating. There are good guys on there, you just have to weed out the bad ones like you would anywhere else—at church, at the club, wherever you meet men."

Sherry nodded. "I haven't given up. My account is still active. I just hadn't paid much attention to matches or messages in a long time because of Stan. Since he and I didn't work out, I guess I'll continue exploring my options."

"If you ladies are finished talking about your dating life, maybe we can get back to work now?" Alex stood in the doorway.

How long had he been standing there? How much had he heard?

"Excuse me. Off to lunch," Gina murmured. She slid past Alex, who shut the door with a firm flick of the wrist. Agitation rolled off him.

Sherry ignored his foul mood and the way her skin prickled with him in the room. "I printed out the copies of all of the accounts, as you requested." Her eyes followed him as he came toward her, using the same smooth, confident walk he always did.

"This is everything?" Alex frowned at the sheets of paper. Using his thumb, he fanned through the pages. Sherry's eyes focused on his big hands, which had palmed her bottom and squeezed her breasts, and that broad thumb that she'd sucked on Friday night.

She shivered with lust. "Yes, that's everything," she said in a low tone.

Alex thumbed the pages again, keeping his gaze downcast. "I

thought you'd wait a while before you jumped back into dating again."

"Why would I do that?"

His gaze lifted to hers, and from the light coming through the window, she saw the flecks of brown and green that fought for dominance in his eyes.

"Don't." The word seemed to be torn out of him.

"Don't what?"

Alex fully faced her, eyes blazing with some emotion. "Don't do it."

Energy vibrated in the room. He clearly wanted to say more, but held back.

"You have no right to tell me what to do, Alex."

"You think I don't know that?"

"You said—"

"I damn well know what I said." One hand fisted at his side. "Believe me. I think about it every day that we're together, when we're not together, when you look at me, when you *breathe* in my direction. I think about the fact that I can't touch you. That *I* created the rules. Rules that I'm finding very difficult to live by."

Her nipples hardened against her blouse. Every word he spoke was a reminder of what she felt toward him—a powerful attraction that had only grown more intense since they'd slept together. If they hadn't slept together, being near him would not be so untenable, but every time he moved, she wanted to reach for him. Every time he spoke, she ached to hear his voice, husky and low in her ear, whispering in a seductive mixture of English and Spanish.

He walked by her, and Sherry remained in the same spot, motionless. She pressed a hand to her stomach. The need for him had become a physical pain, and hearing him speak so openly about his desire made her want to speak her mind.

"We don't have to tell anyone. No one has to know." She was so horny that she wanted to beg him, but instead held her breath and waited in the silence.

She didn't hear Alex move, but was attuned to him and knew the moment he came to stand behind her.

"I can't stop thinking about you," he said in a husky voice. "You're constantly on my mind. The way you taste, the way you smell. Another man touching you the same way I have...I can't tolerate the thought."

His hands rested on her hips and pulled her back into his body. He nudged aside her hair with his nose and pressed his mouth to the side of her neck. Sherry let out a sigh of relief. Closing her eyes, she tilted her head back and gave him access to the length of her throat.

He nibbled on her ear and slid his hands up her abdomen to her breasts. Sherry released an audible breath through her parted lips and reaching back, she caressed his neck and up into his hair. She hadn't been allowed to touch him for what seemed like an eternity but had only been days. She'd never known need like this. She'd never wanted any man like this.

One hand remained on her left breast, a finger rubbing the hard nipple, while the other hand went up her skirt and pushed aside her lace underwear.

His fingers teased the slick folds, and her knees almost buckled.

"Is this because of me?" he rasped.

She turned in his arms, and they kissed hungrily, their tongues fighting in a sloppy, messy kiss. She caressed his hard chest and the ridges of his abdomen, sliding restlessly over his shirt in a desperate need for more.

Everything about him turned her on. The texture of his skin. The clean, masculine scent of his cologne.

"I want you. I want you now," he whispered. He slid his hands up and down the curve of her hips and thighs.

Cupping his face in his hands, Sherry looked deeply into his eyes. "Yes."

Nothing further needed to be said. He backed her against the wall with frantic caresses and frantic kissing, sucking, licking. The sounds they made were toned-down moans so no one could hear.

Sherry reached for his belt. Clumsily, she worked on his pants, releasing the buttons and lowering the zipper as he bared her breasts for his lips and teeth.

Without prompting, she dragged her skirt up past her hips and dropped her panties. When he set her on the credenza, she spread her legs. He entered with a quick thrust, and the satisfaction of being joined to him again brought tears to her eyes.

The truth hit her with the force of a punch. This was why she'd insisted on working with him though he'd tried to give her an out. She'd wanted him to fuck her again.

The sexual frustration from being in such close proximity had reached volcanic levels. Now she was getting exactly what she wanted. Heat. Fire.

They were both so consumed with lust they hadn't even bothered to lock the door.

"Oh god, Alex," she whimpered.

He grunted with each powerful advance of his hips. Sherry curled her fingers into his lush hair, biting her bottom lip and tasting the tinny flavor of blood. All to keep from screaming as she succumbed to an explosive climax that made her see stars.

❧ 7 ❧

Sherry pulled into the driveway of her friend's house, sandwiched between two other homes on a quiet street. She still glowed from spending the night before with Alex. The sex in his office had simply been an appetizer. After work, he'd followed her home, and they'd ordered in a meal and made love again.

Compared to Alex, her other lovers had simply been adequate. She'd had no idea what she'd been missing. Sex with Alex was sensual and cataclysmic. She couldn't stop thinking about their passionate coming together and how absolutely uninhibited she became in his arms.

Sherry marched up to the front door of the two-story Neocolonial. Balancing a pink box of Heavenly Doughnuts in one hand, she rang the doorbell. Seconds later, the door opened.

"Hey!" Shawna greeted Sherry with a bright smile and pulled her into a warm embrace. They'd become good friends as a result of the volunteer work they did with Sunshine Volunteers.

"I come bearing gifts." Sherry handed over the box to her friend.

Shawna glided it under her somewhat pointy nose. "You're too good to me."

They laughed, and Sherry followed Shawna's long ponytail down the hall into a large kitchen with pine cabinets and marble countertops.

"Hey there." Talia, Shawna's best friend, hopped down from a barstool at the island. She was petite, dark-skinned, with a regal bearing and thick, long hair braided and styled in a cute updo. She'd come across as cool and aloof when they originally met, but now that she knew her better, Sherry suspected that had simply been shyness.

"Are the kids already gone?" Sherry asked, pouting her disappointment.

Both Shawna and Talia were in their thirties and married with five children between them. Shawna had two boys and a girl, and Talia had one boy and one girl. Their husbands had agreed to take the kids for the afternoon, which allowed the three of them to indulge in doughnuts and girl talk for a few hours.

"You just missed them. Stay for dinner, and you'll get to see them," Shawna said.

"I might do that," Sherry replied.

Shawna set small plates on the counter for each of them. "Catch us up on everything that's been going on. Was Stan even better in person than on the phone?"

Sherry sat on a stool next to Talia. "Um, not so much. The date was good and bad."

"Uh-oh," Talia murmured.

"Stan never showed."

Her friends gasped.

"He stood you up?" Shawna asked.

Sherry nodded, sliding a plate of Oreo-covered doughnut to her side of the counter and picking up a fork. "Yes, but that wasn't necessarily all bad. Don't get me wrong, it was awful to get stood up. I was embarrassed but fully intended on having dinner alone.

Then I ran into someone from my office and we ended up eating together."

"Okay, this sounds very interesting." Talia ate her Nutella-covered doughnut with her fingers, watching Sherry closely.

"You know who he is. I've talked about him ad nauseam," Sherry said.

Talia frowned at first, then her eyes lit up. "Wait a minute, the Colombian? Your boss, Alex?"

"Hmm. This sounds like it might get interesting," Shawna said.

Both she and Talia knew about Sherry's attraction to Alex, and they knew how guilty she felt about being in a relationship while longing for another man.

"Yes, I had dinner with my boss, Alex."

"How did that go? What happened?" Talia forgot all about her food and focused her attention on Sherry.

"We talked for hours. We shut the restaurant down, and then…"

"And then…" Shawna leaned closer, over the counter.

"We spent the night in a hotel." Sherry hid her face as squeals erupted in the kitchen. "That wasn't the only time," she went on. "We hooked up at work—which I never, ever thought I'd do. And last night he came to my house. We had dinner and hooked up again."

"You *finally* snagged him after crushing on him and wondering if he was interested or not," Talia said.

"Sounds like he was *very* interested," Shawna said.

The three of them laughed again, but then Sherry fell silent.

"What's wrong? What's that look about?" Shawna asked.

"I don't know. I don't want to overthink this."

"I'm the queen of overthinking. What's going through your mind?"

Sherry set down her fork. "I like him a lot, and I'm not sorry about any of the times we slept together. I just…I don't know, wonder if he actually likes me or if it was just sex for him."

For Sherry, each time they'd had sex hadn't only been a physical connection. The emotional connection had been equally consuming. How often did that kind of thing happen? Not often, she was certain.

Shawna sipped lemon-infused water, a frown lining her brow. "How did you leave it between the two of you after last night?"

"It's hard to say. Open-ended, I guess. We didn't make any promises to each other or even discuss what we were doing. We were just going with the flow." But Sherry had woken up this morning and recognized that her feelings were much deeper than mere physical attraction. She wanted Alex in her life in a permanent way but didn't have a clue what his expectations were.

"Listen, there's no point in tossing this around in your head. If nothing else happens, you had a couple of great nights with a man you're attracted to and like a lot." Shawna shrugged.

"Will work be awkward?" Talia asked.

"It was after last week," Sherry said. "There was so much tension between us."

"There's always been tension between you," Talia said dryly.

Sherry laughed. "True, but it was worse. And after yesterday, I'm not sure what to expect from him, and we just started working on a big project together."

Sherry's phone rang. She didn't recognize the number and almost didn't answer, but then she thought that it might not be a telemarketer or some random phone call. What if it was Alex?

She hit the answer button right before the call went to voicemail. "Hello?"

"Hi, Sherry."

It was Alex!

"Hi." His voice immediately dropped low. "I don't know what's happening to me. I haven't stopped thinking about you. For the second weekend in a row, I wasn't a very good visitor at the hospital."

"You weren't?" She mouthed, *It's him*, to her friends.

Their eyes widened.

"No, I wasn't," Alex replied. "I need to see you again."

In his low, accented voice, those words went straight to her core. Her fingers clenched the phone. "You need to see me again?" she repeated for the benefit of her friends, who hung on every word. "When?"

"Tonight. Are you free?"

In the past, she might have pretended that his invitation was too last-minute even if she didn't have plans, but she wanted to see Alex just as much as he clearly wanted to see her, and didn't waste time with games.

"Yes. I'm free tonight." *I'm free every night for you.*

"Great. Can I pick you up at say…eight o'clock?"

"Yes. What do you have planned?"

He chuckled, and the sound excited and aroused her. "That's for me to know and you to find out. Oh, are you afraid of heights?"

"What do you have planned?" she asked again, this time with alarm in her voice.

"What did I just tell you?"

She bit the corner of her lip, smiling hard at her friends, whose curious, wide-eyed expressions demanded more details. "I hate secrets."

"You'll have to suffer through this one. Now answer the question."

She sighed with exaggerated annoyance. "No, I'm not afraid of heights."

"Perfect. I'll pick you up tonight at eight."

As soon as the call ended, Talia said, "Well…?"

"I'm going out with him again. Tonight."

"That much we gathered."

"He wouldn't tell me where we're going or what we'll be doing, so I have no details. I guess I won't see the kids after all. I'll have to skip dinner tonight."

"That doesn't seem to bother you much," Shawna pointed out with a smile.

Sherry couldn't stop grinning. "It doesn't bother me at all."

❧ 8 ❧

Sherry skipped down the steps of her apartment building and straight into Alex's arms. He lifted her off the ground like she weighed a mere ounce and planted a wet kiss on her lips. He tasted delicious, like the most decadent dessert, and she wouldn't have let him go, but he set her down on her feet, and she reluctantly dropped her arms.

"You look amazing," he said, taking her by the hands and simply staring at her in appreciation from head to toe.

She grinned broadly, because who wouldn't when a man looked at you like that? She was glad she'd chosen her long-sleeved, floral-print maxi dress. The flowy dress covered her from chest to ankle, but the off-the-shoulders design made her feel sexy.

"Thank you. And so do you." He wore black on black this evening, and the short sleeves of the polo shirt showed off his muscular forearms covered in fine hairs.

He led her to the Porsche and she slid in. Alex climbed in the driver side and started the car.

"Are you going to tell me what we're going to do, or is that still top secret?" she asked.

"Still top secret." He glanced behind him as he reversed, and she admired his handsome profile. How did she get so lucky?

"Not even a hint?" Sherry whined.

"Not even a hint." He tapped her chin and pulled into traffic.

"Can you at least tell me if I'm dressed appropriately?"

His gaze skipped over her exposed shoulders. "Your dress is very appropriate," he said in a low voice.

A tingle of pleasure swept down her spine. Satisfied with that answer, Sherry settled in for the ride. They remained silent for a bit as they took off toward downtown.

"How was your visit with your friend at the hospital?" she asked.

"Much of the same." He switched lanes.

"How often do you go?"

"Several times a week and every Saturday."

His devotion astounded her. "What's wrong with him?" she asked.

"Her. Her name's Heather, and she has Castleman's disease." When she frowned, he continued. "It's a rare disease that almost killed her a couple of years ago. She's been in and out of the hospital ever since, and about a month ago was admitted again because of another episode." As he talked, his face grew taut.

"I'm sorry. I hope she recovers soon."

"I do too."

Sherry squeezed his hand atop the gearshift, and he smiled gratefully at her.

"She's a good friend. She and Rashad and I have known each other since college. Seeing her sick like this has been a real blow. I'm used to her being vivacious and outgoing, but now she's a fraction of herself, and it's hard. She *will* get better. I know she will."

"I'll keep her in my prayers."

Their gazes met. "Thank you."

From that point on, they talked until they arrived at the tallest

Winthrop Hotel in the city. When the valet took his keys, Alex reached for Sherry's hand and led her inside the hotel.

"I suppose now is a good time to tell you what I have planned."

They stepped into the elevator, still holding hands, which she didn't mind at all. She welcomed his touch and the easy affection he displayed toward her in such a short time.

"When we had dinner at La Tavola, you told me there were parts of the city you hadn't seen and wished to go on a tour. Well, we're going to do that tonight. I'm taking you on a helicopter ride."

"I've never been in a helicopter before," she said excitedly.

"Are you up for it?"

"Hell yes!"

He laughed and pulled her closer with one arm and dropped a kiss on her lips. "You're just what I needed, you know that?" He let out a heavy breath. "I've dealt with some difficult situations in the past year, but in a very short time you've made everything better."

Sherry cupped his cheek. "I could easily say the same about you." She bit her lip, and he bent his head and swiped his tongue across the same place she'd bitten. Mothlike fluttering entered her belly, and she leaned into him.

Honestly sharing how they made each other feel was an important step, and one Sherry felt confident making because she trusted Alex in a way that she hadn't been able to trust a man in a long time. She'd made Stan wait almost three months, going back and forth via text and talking on the phone, before she finally agreed to meet him in person. Even with taking such care, he'd still let her down.

She knew without a doubt that Alex would not let her down.

They exited onto the rooftop and were greeted by the pilot, an older guy with a buzzcut and crooked nose that looked like it had been broken more than once in his lifetime. After signing a waiver, they received instructions and then boarded the black helicopter.

Alex and Sherry sat in the back, strapped in, and the pilot handed them headsets to muffle the noise and facilitate conversation.

Upon takeoff, Sherry clutched Alex's hand, and he kissed her knuckles reassuringly. After a few minutes, she relaxed as they glided through the night sky, over buildings dotted with square and rectangular windows filled with light.

They soared over Highway 285 and circled the blue glass towers of the iconic King and Queen buildings, constructed to resemble chess pieces. The pilot pointed out landmarks such as the governor's mansion, the winding Chattahoochee River, and Stone Mountain in the distance. They soared over upscale neighborhoods like Buckhead, with its high-rise buildings and expansive mansions, as well as lesser-known communities with tree-lined streets and nearby parks.

The tour lasted an hour, and when it was completed, Sherry wished they had another hour to spend in the air. As dates went, it was one of the most memorable and informative, as the pilot provided them with details about Atlanta she'd previously been ignorant about.

She and Alex said their goodbyes and got back into the elevator.

"That was fantastic!" She flung her arms around Alex's neck and planted a juicy kiss on his lips.

He pulled her in tight and backed her into a corner of the cabin. "I love your enthusiasm. If this is my reward, we'll have to do this every weekend."

He kissed her neck, and Sherry's husky laugh filled the small space. Their lips touched again, and she moaned and sighed happily. Kissing and touching Alex was quickly becoming her favorite thing to do.

When the elevator doors opened, they reluctantly pulled apart and exited onto the first floor. Alex had made a reservation in the hotel's restaurant for a late-night dinner, so they made their way there and sat side by side in a funky orange C-shaped booth.

After the waiter took their orders, Alex slipped an arm around Sherry, and she snuggled up next to him.

"What prompted you and Rashad to start Newmark Advisors?" she asked.

Absently, Alex rubbed his palm up and down her arm. "It was actually Rashad who broached the subject. He said it as a joke, but there was always a restlessness in him, and I liked the idea. We were working for an investment firm, making good money, but after some thought, we agreed that starting our own business wasn't such a crazy idea. Like me, he doesn't have any family that he can count on. We'd both been on our own for so long that working for someone else didn't sit well with us. We wanted to be in charge of our own destiny. We discussed our options, pored over the numbers, and made a plan."

Sherry had always had her parents' support, so she couldn't fathom having to fend for herself at a young age. Even now, she knew that if she lost her job or any other tragedy befell her, she had her parents or extended family to depend on.

"You and Rashad are very close."

Alex nodded. "I love him like a brother. I trust him with my life."

"Few people can say that," she said.

"I mean it, and I know he feels the same way about me." He took her hand in his, and a thoughtful frown creased his brow. "Sherry, no matter what happens, I hope you know how important you are to me."

"Whatever happens?" She laughed a little. "You're already breaking us up?" Her stomach tightened in apprehension.

Alex seemed to be in deep thought as he rubbed a thumb across her fingers. "Not at all. But life is so complicated, and sometimes you do what you think is right, but it creates problems later. I want you to know that I care about you. I have for some time, but getting to know you outside of work has convinced me you're exactly the kind of woman I've been looking for."

Sherry touched his face, letting her fingertips brush the fine hairs on his jaw. "I know what you mean. You're exactly the kind of man I've been looking for."

"I'm not perfect."

"I'm not looking for perfect, and I'm sure you're not either. We just click, right?" There was something in his eyes, something he wasn't saying that made her doubt for a minute. There seemed to be a hidden meaning in his words, and though her intuition prompted her to dig deeper, apprehension kept her from doing so.

"Yes, we click. And I want to see more of you. Much more."

"I'd like to see much more of you, too," she said softly.

He kissed her then, and this kiss was without passion or sexual undertones. It was more about affection and sealing their words with finality. She wanted him and he wanted her, and as far as Sherry was concerned, nothing else mattered.

❦

ALEX CAME OUT OF THE BATHROOM AND WALKED ACROSS THE FLOOR to the bed. He and Sherry had spent the day together, and he didn't look forward to the start of the workweek tomorrow, when they'd enter the office and have to pretend they didn't know each other on an intimate level. She was the first woman he'd invited into his home in a long time, and he already felt she belonged here.

He slid under the covers and slipped an arm around her waist. She moaned and turned into his arms.

"You wore me out, *hombre*," she whispered.

He laughed softly. "*Hombre*, eh?"

"Mhmm. I'm learning Spanish now."

"Don't get in too deep. You'll know more than I do, and then I'll have to catch up."

Sherry rubbed one hand up and down the hair on his chest. She was quiet for a moment, and he silently watched her and she watched him.

"I love spending time with you," she whispered.

There was that openness and honesty again.

"I love spending time with you, too." He would spend every day with her if he could.

A hand came to rest over his rapidly beating heart. "A lot. I've never felt this way before."

"Neither have I."

She smiled sweetly and snuggled closer, closing her eyes. "I'm starting to think the best thing that ever happened to me was getting stood up." Alex stroked his fingers through her soft hair, detangling the strands. "Mmm. That feels so good," she murmured.

Tell her now.

But he couldn't. Honesty would spoil the moment. He would lose the warmth of her body against his and the weight of her soft leg thrown over his thigh.

Not yet. He squeezed her closer.

Moments later, her quiet breathing signaled she'd fallen asleep, and Alex eased back to look at her face.

What the hell was he going to do? The longer he delayed, the harder it would be to confess. And how could he? He couldn't risk the fallout.

And he was starting to think he'd already fallen in love with her.

✣ 9 ✣

lex and Sherry worked together in Alex's office. Laptops, notepads, and a multitude of papers were spread out on the round table, his credenza, and his desk. Many of the Ovation employees postponed their appointments until this week, which meant more meetings this week than during the last two combined.

As Alex plugged numbers into an online program, Sherry brought a printout from the credenza over to him.

"I'm going to give you this guy." She set the sheet filled with two pie charts and numbers in front of him. "He has an aggressive approach and would benefit from working with you, I think."

He glanced at the sheet. "You're right. He'd be a perfect candidate for a couple of technology and international stocks that are doing really well right now." He placed the client in the pile with others he intended to share similar stock tips with.

"Agreed."

Sherry moved to walk back to her side of the table, but Alex took her by the hand and tugged her closer. He pressed her palm to his lips, and she smiled warmly at him.

"You have plans tonight?" he asked. So much had changed in

the past few weeks since dinner at La Tavola. Being with Sherry always lifted his spirits and put him in a good mood.

"If I didn't know better, I'd say you want to spend every spare moment with me," she teased.

"And you'd be right," Alex teased back.

He pulled her onto his lap, and her soft bottom landed on his thighs, evoking a surge of heat in his loins. While they managed to get work done today, they also veered off course, like now, because he couldn't resist touching her.

Sherry pouted. "I would love to see you this evening, but I'm meeting with my volunteer group to decide which new projects we want to tackle this quarter."

"Well, I suppose I can give you a break tonight, since we did spend the weekend together."

They'd spent more than the weekend together. Over the past week, they'd spent almost every night after work in each other's company. On Saturday, she'd joined him on a hike up Kennesaw Mountain, and then they ate breakfast at a coffee shop before parting ways so he could go visit his friend in the hospital.

Sunday, they went to a baseball game and then went back to his house, where he taught her how to make a traditional Colombian dish, *bistec a caballo*, over rice. The steak was served topped with a fried egg and *hogao*, a Colombian creole sauce made from scallions and tomatoes, both of which grew in pots on his patio.

"How gracious of you to give me time off," Sherry said, looping her arms around his neck. Her hooded gaze met his.

"I'm a generous man." His gaze shifted. "You have something in your hair."

Sherry brushed at the strands.

"Let me." He removed a piece of shredded paper from her hair and showed it to her. "Got it."

"How in the world did that get in there?"

He chuckled. "Did you bend down toward the shredder?"

"No." She slapped his chest.

"Then I have no idea, *amor*." He trailed the tips of his fingers through her hair. "Your hair smells different. Usually it smells more like mint, but today it smells…fruity."

"I tried a different shampoo and conditioner. Very observant, Señor Barraza." She rolled her Rs extra hard.

"Look at you. We're going to have you speaking Spanish yet."

"Maybe you can teach me a word a day."

"We'll start with the nasty ones," he said.

"Of course you would say that." She nuzzled his neck. "I think the new products make my hair softer. What do you think?"

He grasped a handful of her tresses. "It's hard to tell. All of you is so soft all the time." He nipped her chin with his lips.

"Keep talking like that, and you might get yourself laid at work."

"Again? In that case—"

Two quick knocks on the door, and Sherry jumped up from his lap. Dammit.

Rashad poked his head in. He glanced between them as Sherry edged farther away from Alex.

"Hey, hope I didn't interrupt anything." Rashad came fully into the office. "Wanted to see if you still want to grab lunch together."

"Sure." Alex glanced at his watch. He'd lost track of the time. "We can get back to work after lunch," he said to Sherry, keeping his voice neutral.

She nodded, careful not to give even the slightest hint of what they'd been up to only moments before.

"Care to join us?" Rashad asked.

"No, thanks." She picked up her notepad and a few files. "I'm going back to my own office to make a few phone calls before I leave for lunch myself. Alex, I'll see you later this afternoon."

She exited and quietly closed the door.

Rashad turned slowly to face Alex and shoved his hands into his pockets, rolling back onto the balls of his feet. "Why do I get the feeling I interrupted something?"

Alex tapped the eraser end of a pencil on the stack of papers before him. "That's your imagination."

"Don't bullshit a bullshitter. This is me, and it's not like you didn't already tell me my absence at La Tavola got you laid."

"That doesn't change the fact that you owe me a steak dinner."

"Come on, man. You should be taking me out to dinner, as a thank you."

"Of course you'd see it that way," Alex said dryly, though he didn't completely disagree. If not for Rashad, he'd still be in the same work, home, hospital cycle before Sherry became a part of his life and changed his outlook.

Rashad had bailed on him after one of his out-of-town lady friends flew in unexpectedly and asked to see him. Over the years, Alex had come to realize the importance of women in Rashad's life. Chocolate-skinned and with a smile worthy of a toothpaste ad, Rashad looked like the kind of guy who should be headlining movies. He parlayed his good looks and flamboyant dress—a diamond in each ear, and today a dark red pinstriped suit that only he could pull off—into the bedrooms of more women than Alex could keep track of.

"So the two of you still pretending you're not together?" Rashad asked, as Alex stood.

"That's the way she wants it."

"You mean that's the way you want it."

Alex closed his computer and gave his friend his undivided attention. "It's for the best, for both of us. For now."

"And how long are you planning to keep this secret? The two of you have been running around town together, going on helicopter rides and hiking and shit, and then you come into the office and pretend there's nothing going on."

"It hasn't been that long."

"Your head's been messed up since the first night you spent with her. Not to mention you've been carrying a boner for her ever since you hired her."

"You're exaggerating." Alex went behind his desk and grabbed his jacket off the back of the chair. As he slipped his hands through the sleeves, Rashad crossed his arms and looked at him like a disapproving father.

"I have never seen you like this, not once, over any woman. Before you even slept with her, all you did was talk about how sweet she was and her smile and all that shit. Come on, Alex. How do you really feel about her? Because you're right, she's sweet. She's a good woman. She's not playing games, and you have to know that, because I can see it just by the way she carries herself in the office."

Alex absorbed the truth of Rashad's words and sank onto the edge of the desk.

"She's the One," he answered without reservation or embarrassment. He'd had plenty of time to consider his feelings, and he had no doubt that Sherry was the woman he'd been looking for all along. The reason every other relationship didn't work. He wanted to lock her down. He wanted to make her his until the end of time.

Rashad's eyebrows rose. He might have suspected that Alex had feelings for Sherry, but he didn't expect them to run so deep.

"Tell me you're kidding, bruh. The One? No such thing exists. That's some nonsense women invented to tie us down. Besides"—his voice lowered—"there's that little situation with you and Heather."

Alex immediately sobered. "I know." He ran a weary hand down his face.

"I can't tell you what to do—"

"Since when?" They'd known each other since they were eighteen years old, and just like blood brothers behaved, neither was known for holding his tongue.

Rashad chuckled. "Okay, I can tell you what to do, but that doesn't mean you'll listen." He stuffed his hands into his pockets again, a serious expression on his face. "Listen man, Sherry seems great, and maybe what you feel for her is genuine."

"It is genuine," Alex said firmly.

"Well, like I said, I've never seen you like this."

"I've never felt like this."

Rashad held up his hands in surrender. "Okay, fine. So if you really think she's the One, you know what you need to do."

"Yes. I know." Alex rubbed the back of his neck.

He needed to be honest and upfront, but the situation had already gotten out of hand. Their relationship had been unexpected and moved so fast. How could he tell Sherry the truth now? Maybe he'd become too cynical, but she was the one bright spot in a world he sometimes wanted to burn to the ground.

"Bite the bullet," Rashad advised. "She might understand."

"Maybe."

"You can't not tell her."

"You think I don't know that?" Alex snapped.

"Then what are you doing?" Rashad snapped back. "You've always been honest and upfront with women, and most of them didn't care. What's different—"

"She is!" Alex glared at his friend. "She is," he said in a calmer voice. "That's the difference. It's her. I don't want to lose her if I tell her the truth. Because she might not understand."

Whether she did or not, Alex couldn't deny he needed to tell Sherry everything. Rashad was right that she deserved to know.

But if he told her, would she understand?

❧ 10 ❧

"**Y**ou met someone."

Alex stopped in the middle of fluffing the pillows behind Heather's head. Her long blonde hair had long ago lost its luster, and her pale blue eyes no longer sparkled. Yet she managed a smile that gave him a small measure of hope that maybe all was not lost. That maybe everything the doctors had subjected her to over the past couple of years—the steroids, the surgery, the medicines and experimental drugs—was not in vain. He hoped that one day soon he'd be walking her out the exit doors, into the car, and away from this place for good.

"How did you know?"

"Aside from the fact that I don't see you as often? Rashad."

"Rashad talks too much."

"Tell me about her."

Alex hesitated. He no longer discussed his love life with Heather. He'd stopped because he didn't want her to think the reason he hadn't pursued a relationship with anyone else was because of her. She didn't need that burden of guilt on top of everything else she had to deal with. He silently cursed at Rashad for even mentioning Sherry to Heather.

"It's nothing," he said.

"Well, if it's nothing, then you should have no problem telling me about her." Heather's voice had grown firm, the way it always did when she pushed back against something he and Rashad thought was best for her.

He sat on the side of the bed. "My love life is none of your concern."

"Since when?" she asked.

"You need to concentrate on getting better, so we can get you out of this—"

"Stop it." She was no longer joking and took a tremulous breath. "You know that's not going to happen."

Her words gutted him. She couldn't give up. Not when she'd managed to survive several near-death episodes with this dreaded disease. Eight months ago the doctors had told them to prepare for organ failure and death, but she'd proved them wrong and was still here. He couldn't allow her to give up.

"Of course you're going to get out of here. It's only a matter of time. You have to have faith and stay positive."

"It took them too long to figure out what was wrong with me," Heather said.

Her first episode had occurred a couple of years ago, and Alex and Rashad had flown to Texas to find out what was going on. She'd responded well to steroids and was released from the hospital, but when the second episode hit only a month later, treatment by a drug used for leukemia had been the only way to save her.

By then, the damage had been done. She'd lost vision in one eye and suffered from kidney failure. Months later, she was in the hospital again, that episode making one of her lungs useless and causing a series of small strokes that made her more frail.

Alex took her hand and squeezed. "But now that we know what's wrong, they can help you. That's why Rashad and I brought you here. So you can get the care of a doctor who specializes in this disease. Don't you dare give up."

Heather's head lolled to the side so she could look out the

window. He'd never seen her so despondent, and her lack of response ate at him. A few years ago she'd been energetic, fun-loving, and on top of the world. In a short time, she'd lost her enthusiasm, grown tired and lethargic. And there wasn't a damn thing he could do about it.

Rashad walked in holding two cups of coffee. "This is pretty good coffee," he said, handing one to Alex. "They've got a gourmet coffee shop down there, but I brought you a plain coffee." He went to the other side of the bed and sat down.

"He won't tell me about his new girlfriend," Heather said. "So why don't you tell me?"

Rashad glanced at Alex. "Oh, he's a goner, Heather," he said with a grin.

"You mean there's a woman alive who has captured the heart of our brooding Colombian heartthrob?" she teased.

"You heard it here first," Rashad said.

"Both of you can stop now, anytime you're ready." Alex sipped his coffee. Rashad was correct. The coffee wasn't bad at all. He set the Styrofoam cup on the table beside the bed and listened to Rashad give a rundown of his relationship with Sherry.

Occasionally, Heather asked questions, and when Alex thought Rashad was exaggerating, he interjected a correction to the narrative. The three of them laughed and talked like they always did when they came together. Eventually, the conversation shifted to Rashad and the stream of women who went through the revolving door of his home. That gave Alex a chance to turn the tables and give him a hard time.

Finally, Heather shook her head and laughed. "You're never going to change, are you?"

"Why change when nothing's wrong?" Rashad asked.

Alex noted Heather's tired expression. Her eyes drooped and she stifled a yawn. They'd worn her out. He stood. "Time for us to get out of here, Rashad."

His friend nodded, getting to his feet, too.

"No, you guys can stay." Heather reached out her hands to them.

"Nah, Alex is right. You look tired, babe. You know we'll be back again in the next day or two." Rashad bent down and kissed her on the forehead.

She took his hand in hers, and the mood in the room shifted. The air became heavy with regret and unspoken words.

Heather's gaze connected with Alex's, and she extended her hand to him as well. He took it but didn't want to hear what she was about to say, yet knew he couldn't stop her.

"I love you guys so much," Heather said thickly.

Rashad glanced away out the window, as if he couldn't bear to look at her.

Tears filled Heather's eyes. "I couldn't be loved more if you were actually my blood. I don't know how I'll ever repay you, but know that I'll do anything within my power that you ask me to do. If I can do it."

"The only thing we want you to do is get better," Alex said.

"I'll do my best." Her smile was wan and sad. "Any woman would be lucky to have either of you. But lucky me, I'm fortunate to have you both in my life. And for that, I'm forever thankful. Whatever happens moving forward, I want you to know how much I appreciate everything you've done for me. The sacrifices you've made."

"It's not over yet," Alex said in a thick voice.

She didn't respond, and the helplessness he always encountered whenever he contemplated her situation beat unrestricted inside his chest.

"I'll see you tomorrow, or the next day. I'll be happy whenever you come. But please don't put your life on hold for me," she said.

A tear slipped from the corner of her eye, and Alex swiped it away with his finger.

"Everything we've done, we've wanted to do. Willingly. Don't you forget that."

"I know. Just another reason for me to love you so much."

Alex kissed her knuckles. "Get some rest."

Moments later, he and Rashad left the room. Neither of them spoke as they walked quietly out of the building and stood under the overhang in silence.

"She's going to make it, right?" Rashad turned to him, his eyes glistening with tears.

Alex stared across the parking lot, watching the people milling around. A steady flow of traffic exited and entered the building through the automatic doors.

He couldn't answer Rashad's question, because he didn't know the answer.

And he didn't want to lie.

❧ II ❧

Whenever Sunshine Volunteers chose the hospital as one of their locations to work, Sherry happily participated. Some of the volunteers didn't like working at the hospital because of the antiseptic smell, and the sight of sick people depressed them. But Sherry saw the environment in a different way. Visiting the hospital was an opportunity to bring joy and positivity into the lives of people who were otherwise distressed by whatever illness forced them to be there.

Today they were delivering the flowers from a celebrity wedding. The bouquets had been table settings in the reception and all over the church, and instead of discarding them, the bride had donated every single one to the group. Taking them to the patients meant they could be reused to brighten someone's day. They were also delivering toys, books, and coloring books to the kids in the children's wing—all collected during a recent donation drive.

Sherry and Shawna covered the hospital, working two two-hour shifts, and Sherry started with the children. After the first two hours, they made their way to the cafeteria for lunch before getting back to work for the last two hours in the afternoon. At that point, they'd swap roles. Shawna would visit with the children, and Sherry would spend time with the adults.

After going through the cafeteria line and getting their food, they sat down across from each other.

"Hospital food has come a long way," Shawna remarked.

"It has." Sherry dipped her fork into a mountain of chicken-fried rice. Today's theme was Chinese food. Shawna had chosen sweet and sour chicken.

"How were the kids?" Shawna asked.

"Wonderful, as usual. I'm always amazed at how much of a great attitude they have, you know? One little boy was so thankful for the coloring book I gave him, he insisted on giving me a hug. Even though he was in pain, poor baby. It broke my heart, but made me happy at the same time."

She had been volunteering for years. Service had been instilled in her by her parents ever since she was little and joined them and other church members for the annual Thanksgiving food drive, serving meals to people who lived in the community surrounding the church. The bravery of the children Sherry met always amazed her, even back then, and how they managed to stay upbeat and keep a positive outlook in some of the most dire circumstances. They were her favorite group to work with because of how their little faces lit up when they received their gifts.

"Children are amazingly resilient," Shawna agreed. "I'm genuinely surprised at how much strength they can have, but I think part of that strength is drawn from us, the adults. If they see that we're positive, they feed off that energy. I've noticed it with my own kids. If Ryan and I are upset with each other or for what-ever reason or not our usual affectionate selves, the kids notice. They'll even try to cheer us up by climbing into our laps or doing something silly to make us laugh."

Sherry listened intently to her friend, imagining the day when she and Alex would have children of their own. They weren't long into their secret relationship, but it didn't seem far-fetched to think about a future with him. She already imagined them married and sharing a bed every night.

They were in sync in every way, but at times she wondered if the speed with which they'd come together overwhelmed him. *She* wasn't overwhelmed. She'd harbored feelings for him for a long time, so it was a relief to finally be open about it.

She suspected he felt some of what she did. At times she caught him staring at her or sensed he wanted to say something but held back. One day he would reveal his innermost thoughts, and she would, too.

Her phone beeped, and when she checked the screen, she'd received a text.

Alex: Just left the hospital. Didn't want to bother you. I'll see you tonight.

She frowned. She'd wanted to see him because he told her he would be at the hospital to see his friend Heather.

"What's wrong?" Shawna asked.

"It's a text from Alex."

"Oh, your new man?"

"Yes." Sherry blushed. "I thought I'd see him before he left the hospital, but he's already gone. I wanted to meet his friend, but I'll have to do that another time, I guess."

She'd broached the subject with him because he spent so much time at the hospital visiting Heather. She didn't want to encroach on their relationship, but she'd followed through and prayed for her like she'd promised. For that reason, she wanted to at least meet the woman she prayed for regularly.

"Did he say why he had to leave suddenly?" Shawna sipped her water.

"He didn't."

They ate in silence for a bit.

"Can I ask you something?" Shawna asked.

"Sure."

"If it's none of my business, feel free to tell me. But you've spent a lot of time with Alex, at least based on our conversations."

Sherry set down her fork. "I know where you're going with this. You think we're spending too much time together, that maybe I'm too into him." Her parents had expressed the same concerns. Not only that she and Alex spent a lot of time together, but they worked together and saw each other every day. They worried that she was moving too fast.

"I'm not judging. I just don't want you to get hurt again. How much do you really know about him?"

"Everything I need to know," Sherry said, getting defensive, the way she did when her parents questioned the relationship. They thought this was a rebound thing from Stan, but it wasn't. She took a deep breath and decided to share her feelings with her friend—feelings she hadn't shared with anyone else and hardly wanted to acknowledge herself. "He's everything I've ever wanted in a man. He's kind, honest, sexy, smart, and we have fun together. I think...I think I've fallen in love with him."

"Love?" Shawna didn't sound skeptical. She seemed to want to confirm she'd heard Sherry correctly.

"I know it sounds crazy, but that's how I feel. Like I've already fallen in love with him. We spend several nights a week together, and that doesn't include the fact that we talk at work and text each other multiple times per day. I do wonder if so much contact is overkill, because I don't want to smother him, but he clearly enjoys our conversations as well. At least, he hasn't run off yet."

One corner of Shawna's mouth lifted into a half-smile. "Well, falling in love can happen at any time. You know my story. It happened to me."

She had fallen for her husband, Ryan, after spending only a couple of days with him.

"So you understand. That's how I feel," Sherry said. "And it's not one-sided. I think Alex feels the same way. Maybe he's not *in love* with me." She laughed self-consciously. "But there's something between us. Something strong that makes me miss him when we're apart, for even a few minutes. I want to be with him all the time."

A smile slowly spread across Shawna's lips. "You know what, I'm happy for you. If anyone deserves to be happy with the right man, it's you." She lifted her glass. "I wish you a long and happy relationship. Cheers."

"Cheers." Sherry bumped her can of soda against her friend's glass.

⚜

SHE SHOULDN'T DO THIS. SHE SHOULD MIND HER OWN BUSINESS AND go home. But that wasn't what she did. Call it curiosity or some sort of sixth sense, but there was something odd about Alex's abrupt departure from the hospital.

After delivering the rest of the flowers, Sherry decided to find out which room Heather was in, which was fairly easy to do. Having volunteered at the hospital numerous time, the staff knew her, and there was no other patient at the hospital named Heather with Castleman's disease.

Sherry exited the elevator and walked down the hallway toward the patient's assigned room. At the door, she peeked through the rectangular window and saw a blonde woman asleep inside. A series of machines in the room monitored her vitals and displayed the results for medical staff.

Sherry's heart went out to her. Even in sleep, the strain the disease had taken on her body was obvious. She looked thin and frail, face drawn and pale, long hair limp and unwashed.

Sherry stepped away from the door and bumped into one of the nurses. "Oh, I'm sorry," she said.

The nurse, a middle-aged black woman with a thin build, smiled. Sherry recognized her from previous visits. Her name was Helen.

"No problem. Do you know her?"

"No, I don't. She's a friend of a friend, and I just wanted to peek in and see how she's doing."

"It's been rough, that's for sure." Helen pursed her lips and shook her head.

"I don't know much about Castleman's disease. Do you think she'll be here much longer?"

The nurse winced. "Of course, you know I can't discuss a patient's medical status."

"Of course not! I meant in general. What's the norm?"

Helen let out an audible breath and glanced in at Heather. "Hard to say. It varies by patient. We don't know a whole lot about the disease, and unfortunately, by the time the doctors figured out what was wrong with her and she arrived here to see a specialist, it had advanced aggressively. The disorder attacks the lymph nodes and other organs and for lack of a better phrase, shuts them down. I will say, what's working in her favor is that she has a good support system, and that matters in cases like these. Her friend and her husband come by to see her frequently."

"Oh. I didn't know she was married. I know her friend, though."

"They've both been good about coming to see her regularly. They're her only visitors. I don't think she has anyone else. Frankly, if I had two good-looking men like that coming to see me almost every day, I would stick around, too." Helen laughed softly and nudged Sherry.

"You're terrible, but I know what you mean. So her husband's a looker, too?"

"Oh yes, honey." Helen fanned herself with one hand. "He's beautiful, from somewhere in South America. Colombia, I think. Yes, that's it. He's Colombian."

Sherry went still. "Her husband is Colombian?" That wasn't so crazy that her husband could be Colombian, like Alex, could it? Sherry's pulse ticked higher as she waited for the reply.

"Yes, and he's quite the looker. With thick, dark hair and hazel eyes. *Ooh.* He doesn't smile too often, because you can tell he's upset about seeing his wife in this condition. But when he does, it's like the sun comes out." She sighed and looked heavenward. "I pray I find a man like that for myself. Actually, I'll take either one of those fine men. The Black one or the Spanish one. They're both delicious."

Sherry's thumping pulse slowly transformed into a full-blown panic attack. Helen couldn't be right. "Are you sure that the Colombian is her husband?"

"I'm very sure. He's in here almost every day. Well, in the past couple of weeks, not as much as he used to be, but still fairly often."

"There must be some mistake," Sherry said softly. Dismay seeped into her veins like poison.

The nurse watched her strangely. "There's no mistake. That's her husband. We all know because he's very devoted to her. They both are. But especially him."

Sherry cast a glance inside the room once again and stared at the sleeping woman. Heather was Alex's wife, not his friend? He and Heather were *married*? She suddenly felt dizzy and reached out a steadying hand to the wall.

"Sweetie, are you okay?"

Sherry swallowed hard. She was going to be sick. She was going to be violently ill and throw up the contents of her stomach all over the hospital floor.

"Yes, I'm fine," she said in a shaky voice. "I...I didn't realize they were married." She swallowed hard again.

Helen's eyes turned sympathetic, as if she'd guessed the reason for Sherry's odd response. "Yes, I'm afraid so. They're married," she said quietly.

"Thank you for the information." Sherry backed away. "I...I need to go."

She darted down the hall on legs as stable as soft rubber. When she reached the elevator, she jabbed the down button and the cabin came right away. Two doctors nodded at her as she walked through the open doors, but she didn't acknowledge the greetings.

Instead, she went to stand at the back and rested her shoulder against the wall.

Oh god, oh god. She closed her eyes and pressed a hand to her throbbing temple. No wonder Alex had fought so hard to keep their affair a secret.

All this time, he'd been playing her for a fool.

❧ 12 ❧

*J*ust do it.

Sherry sat on the sofa in Alex's living room, stiff as an iron rod and contemplating her next move. After leaving the hospital, she had run errands and stopped at home to change into jeans and a blouse. The entire time, she'd simply been going through the motions, numbed by the revelation that Alex was married.

During the past few hours, she'd wondered if the nurse could have been wrong. Surely there was a misunderstanding. But Helen had been so certain, and then there was the fact that Alex was very devoted to Heather. Sherry had initially thought his frequent visits demonstrated what a good and devoted friend he was, but now she had to reconsider everything she'd believed about their relationship.

The pain in her head had only magnified on the way over to Alex's condo, and when she saw him, she hadn't known what to say or do. She'd kissed and hugged him as usual, perhaps clinging a bit too much as fear of loss gripped her. Fortunately, he didn't notice, but she paid close attention to him. She'd studied him as he talked, wondering how she couldn't have seen who he really was.

He'd certainly changed from the time they started this relationship. The grim exterior had been replaced with a more affable personality, closer to the man she'd met when she started working at Newmark Investors a couple of years ago. Otherwise, he seemed the same.

Yet she couldn't help but wonder if she'd seen only what she wanted to see because she was so desperate for a relationship. Had she been blinded by her attraction to him?

"Would you like some wine?" Alex called from the kitchen.

He was in the process of making dinner, and the scent of spices filled the air. Normally, the aromas would tempt her appetite, but eating was so far from her mind that she questioned if she could ever tolerate food again. They planned to go to a movie later, an indie film, and one of the rare moments they both agreed because their tastes were so different. She preferred comedies and he preferred dramas. She didn't look forward to the movie, either.

"No, thanks."

Sherry couldn't see him from here, but she heard movement in the kitchen, utensils banging against pots and every now and again the sound of the faucet running as he washed his hands or vegetables. She looked at the room, beautifully decorated in warm tones, with splashes of color in the chair cushions and fake flowers in the middle of the glass coffee table.

Did Heather have a hand in decorating this place? Of course she did.

Sherry walked over to the bookcase that spanned an entire wall, filled with hardcover books and pictures and knickknacks. He read widely, or he and Heather did—nonfiction and commercial fiction like thrillers—with books written in English and Spanish.

She scoured the photos, which she'd only paid cursory attention to before. Most were scenic shots from trips he'd taken over the years, but one frame contained a photo of Alex, Rashad, and Heather, and they appeared to be in Colombia, based on the architecture of the buildings. This was the only photo of her on the shelves. Had he simply wiped out all evidence of her existence to perpetuate his adultery?

Sherry's chest hurt, and she blinked back tears, clamping both hands over her mouth to suppress an anguished whimper. Why hadn't he told her? This explained why he was such a private person and not a soul at work knew the truth. He needed to hide that he was a married man with an ill wife so he could carry on his affairs.

Nausea bubbled in her stomach. "I'm going to use the bathroom."

"Dinner will be ready in fifteen minutes."

Sherry rushed down the hall to the full bath and shut the door, leaning back against it. She took two huge, quivering breaths and waited. Nothing happened. She didn't throw up.

She sank onto the toilet lid and stared at the wall. She needed to independently verify his marriage. Maybe Helen was wrong.

With that idea in mind, she rummaged through the vanity drawers and checked the medicine cabinet. She found the usual items for men—shaving equipment, a box of condoms, and over-the-counter drugs. Nothing incriminating. No evidence of a woman anywhere.

Not satisfied, she left the bathroom and paused in the hallway to listen as Alex continued moving around in the kitchen. He'd turned on some music, and the sounds of a man singing in Spanish in a mellow voice floated back as he worked.

Sherry carefully crept down the hallway to the spare bedroom, which she had never entered before. She left the door ajar so she could hear if Alex started coming down the hall.

At first glance, she didn't see anything damning. The sparsely furnished room contained only a bed and a table with a lamp on it. Sheer curtains covered the windows, and a van Gogh print hung on the wall.

She went to the closet and swung open the double doors. She flicked on the light and her heart plummeted. Women's clothes and shoes filled the walk-in closet. She froze in the doorway, shocked. He'd moved all Heather's personal belongings in here. How callous.

"What are you doing?"

Sherry spun around to face Alex. A frown marred his brow. They stared at each other. "Are you going to make me ask?"

His jaw tightened. "Ask what?"

"Who do these clothes belong to?"

"Sherry…"

Cold with the knowledge that her heart was about to be shattered, Sherry shivered and wrapped her arms around herself. "Do these clothes belong to your wife? Is Heather your wife?"

His eyes pleaded with her. "I can explain."

No, no. Up until that moment, she'd held out hope that maybe she was wrong. This was all a big misunderstanding easily cleared up with a logical explanation she'd simply overlooked. All he'd had to say was no, but he hadn't.

"What is there to explain? You're married, Alex. You're *married*, and we've been sleeping together for the past few weeks. And even worse, your wife is lying in the hospital sick, and you're using me and probably other women to satisfy your twisted lust because she's no longer available. What happened to the words for better or worse, in sickness and in health?"

His eyes widened. "There are no other women, and if you let me explain, you'll understand what all of this means."

He took a step forward, and she sidestepped away from the closet door so she wouldn't get trapped in the interior.

"There is nothing to explain," she said slowly.

"My relationship with Heather is not what it seems. Yes, she's my wife, but in name only."

Sherry laughed shrilly. "Oh well, that makes it okay, then. Carry on cheating on your wife, but you won't be doing it with me." She barged toward the door, but he stepped back and blocked her path. "Get out of my way, Alex."

"Not until you hear me out." He held up his hands, hesitant to touch her but determined to keep her from leaving.

"What could you possibly say to make what you've done okay? You lied to me! You're not a free man."

"In the traditional sense, I *am* free, but technically, no. Heather and I got married because of her illness. She's been in and out of the hospital for the past couple of years. The first few months were crazy, and we thought she would die—me and Rashad. We didn't know what to do or how to help her. I don't remember who got the idea of getting married first—me or Rashad—but we thought it would work because she needed better treatment. I married her and put her on my insurance so she could get the care she needed."

Sherry folded her arms across her chest. "And I'm supposed to believe what you say?"

"It's the truth!"

"Even if it is, that doesn't matter to me. You're *married*, and you kept that information from me. How am I supposed to trust you now?"

His chest moved up and down in a fast rhythm. When he spoke next, he used a calmer, lower voice. "I didn't set out to lie to you. Everything happened so fast between us. We were just supposed to have dinner, and then...and then, in the parking lot, we kissed. I'm not proud of what I did, but I took my chance. Do you know how often I'd fantasized about making love to you? When the opportunity presented itself, I couldn't not take it."

"That still makes you a disgusting liar."

Alex winced. "You have become the most important person in my life. I know that I'm important to you, too. We can get through this."

"You and me, *we*, are not going to do anything. *You* are going to stick to your vows or whatever you promised Heather, and leave me out of it."

He shook his head. "That's not possible."

"What I said is not up for debate."

"I'm not letting you go."

"You don't have a choice!" Sherry marched toward the door,

fully intending to bypass him, but he grabbed her wrist. She tried to jerk away. "Stop."

He grasped both of her arms. Desperation flashed in his eyes. "Listen to me. I was wrong, yes. But Heather and I are not in love. We're not a real married couple."

"I. Don't. Care. You kept your marriage from me and turned me into a woman who's sleeping with a married man. You should have told me everything. Instead, you took the choice away from me as to whether or not I would be okay with this arrangement."

"I can't abandon her," he said. "That's not the kind of man I am."

"I'm not asking you to abandon her. That's not the kind of woman I am. I'm not giving you an ultimatum, Alex. I'm telling you that we're done."

"*No*," he said in a deeper, harsher voice. "This can't be the end. Not for you and me. Not for what I know is between us." A fierce light entered his eyes. "I love you."

Her stomach clenched in agony, and she had the sudden urge to burst into tears. "Don't say that."

His expression softened. "It's true."

"Don't! You want to pretend your marriage doesn't matter, and I can't. Don't you remember what I told you the night we had dinner at La Tavola? Trust, Alex. Trust is the most important part of a relationship for me. I can't trust you now. I don't care about your feelings for me, and I don't care about your reasons for what you did." Her voice thickened as she struggled to get the words out. This had to be the hardest thing she'd ever done. Even harder than accepting the pain of knowing her boyfriend of eighteen months had been cheating on her with someone else. "We're done. Leave me alone. You're married. Be with your wife. Your friend-wife. Whatever arrangement you have. Leave. Me. Alone."

When she pulled away this time, he didn't stop her. She rushed past him out the door, eyes filled with tears and heart demolished by the soul-crushing pain of betrayal.

❧ 13 ❧

He didn't want to be here, pretending to care what these people thought so he could get their business. Alex ran a hand along the inside collar of his tux and then took another sip of beer.

The Johnson Foundation was one of the largest private charitable foundations in the world and made a difference in the lives of many around education, healthcare, and children-focused causes. But he should have bowed out of the invitation to the highbrow reception because he simply wasn't in the mood. He only came because Rashad had insisted they attend, pointing out the event was a good opportunity to meet people with whom they could expand their clientele.

Except Alex had no desire to speak to the rich, famous, or, in some cases, both. All he could think about was the fact that Sherry wouldn't speak to him. Even at work, she refused to give him a minute of her time. He'd managed to corner her in the break room yesterday afternoon and suggest they get together for drinks after work, to talk, but she'd declined.

"I have plans," she said woodenly.

"What about tomorrow?"

"I have plans then, too." She refused to look at him. She gripped the tiny bag of chips in her hand, waiting for him to move aside and let her pass.

"Plans with who?"

"No one you know."

She couldn't have hurt him more if she'd clawed his skin off and left him to bleed out. Had she gone back on Match.com? The thought sent him into a panic.

"Sherry." He reached for her, but she sidestepped him. Jealous anger surged inside him. "It's been one fucking week and you're already seeing someone?"

She glared at him. "What's your point? I'm not allowed to move on?"

No! he wanted to shout. He raked hands trembling with frustration through his hair. He needed her. Even if she never let him touch her again, he simply needed her in his life. She had brought light and happiness in the pitch darkness and then cut him off.

She cleared her throat. "We should probably steer clear of each other. If not, people will talk, and neither of us want there to be any rumors about us. We agreed we didn't want anyone to know about our relationship."

"Then let's meet outside of work. Are you going to pretend you feel nothing? I don't buy that. There was too much passion between us. We fit together perfectly. Don't tell me—"

He broke off when a male employee walked in. His curious eyes settled on how Alex and Sherry were huddled in the corner. The employee nodded before making his way to the vending machine on the other side of the room.

Sherry took that moment to slip away.

"Alex, I have someone you need to meet."

Rashad's voice broke through the memory. He approached with a brown-skinned woman beside him. Her long, thick hair hung in loose waves past her shoulders, and her round face bore a welcoming smile. She was exactly the type of woman Rashad would go for, if it weren't for the rings on her left hand and the fact that she was visibly pregnant.

"This is Simone Brooks. She's the philanthropic ambassador for the Johnson Foundation."

They shook hands.

"Nice to meet you," she said. "Rashad has been telling me all about Newmark Advisors and the work you do. I'm especially appreciative of the donation the two of you made tonight. That money will go a long way toward meeting the basic needs of food and shelter for children in this country." She used perfect diction when she spoke.

Alex concentrated on the conversation at hand, temporarily shoving all thoughts of Sherry from his mind so he could focus.

"Thank you. It's our pleasure to donate. Both Rashad and I believe in giving back, and it's always been our plan to use our company to aid work in areas like this."

They chatted for a while, bonding on their shared South American heritage. Simone's paternal grandmother was Brazilian, and though she'd never visited Colombia, he'd been to Brazil. They discussed a couple of places they were both familiar with in the northern part of the country, and he spoke a few words to her in his limited Portuguese.

By the time she waved goodbye to network with other guests, he'd secured a promise from her to meet at a later date and discuss investment opportunities for her and her husband.

Both he and Rashad watched her walk away, one hand resting over her protruding belly.

"That's what I'm talking about," Rashad said enthusiastically. He turned to Alex with dollar signs in his eyes. "I knew you two would connect well."

"And how did you know that?"

"The South American connection, of course. You know my motto. Find common ground, and you can get people to agree to almost anything."

Anyone overhearing the conversation would mistake Rashad

for a heartless shark. In reality, he cared about his clients but was smart enough to realize that while other advisors saw their clients simply as people they did business with, establishing a rapport encouraged a long-term relationship. In that regard, he and Alex held the same belief.

Alex took another sip of beer.

"What's wrong with you? You haven't been yourself for quite a while. I thought you'd shake out of it a little bit once we got to the reception."

"You know what's wrong with me."

Rashad sighed. "Sherry still won't talk to you?"

"No." Alex tilted back his head and drained the bottle.

"I'm sorry, man. I don't know what to tell you."

"I need to get out of here. I need to go see her."

"Are you sure that's a good idea?" Rashad's brow furrowed.

"I think it's a terrible idea, but I can't just do nothing."

Rashad nodded. "Go. Fix the problem between the two of you, because I don't need your personal problems affecting my money."

Alex couldn't believe he'd heard him correctly. "You're sure?"

"Yes, I'm sure. I got this."

"Thanks." He clapped Rashad on the shoulder. He was a good friend, and no doubt he could handle the reception without Alex. But what made him an even better friend was the fact that he didn't say *I told you so*. He'd warned Alex about telling Sherry everything, and Alex hadn't listened.

Now he needed to fix the mess he'd made.

※

"DARN. THAT'S WHAT YOU GET FOR MOVING AROUND IN THE DARK," Sherry muttered to herself. She flipped on the lamp and sighed at all the popcorn she'd accidentally spilled on the carpet.

She set the bowl on the table beside the sofa and paused the TV. Quickly, she cleaned up the mess and turned out the light again. She pulled the blanket around her body, set the bowl of popcorn on her lap, and resumed binge-watching the comedy show.

She needed the escape and the ability to laugh. She hadn't laughed much in the past week ever since she learned about Alex's deception.

She understood his desire to help his friend but found it hard to forgive that he'd kept such an important aspect of his life from her, and he'd had ample opportunity to tell everything. She was hurt and disappointed that he hadn't lived up to her expectations, and embarrassed because of how much she'd gushed to her friends about him.

She'd been better off by herself, stress-free, and needed to get back to that state.

A loud knock sounded on the door. "Sherry!"

Her heart jumped. Alex. She muted the TV and sat frozen, as if he could see through the walls, but wouldn't notice her if she remained still.

"I know you're in there. I saw the light in your window from downstairs. Open the door. I don't care who you have in there. Tell him to come the door. Tell him to face me!" His words slurred slightly and his accent sounded thicker.

"Go away, Alex!"

"I will not. I will not leave until you open the door."

Sherry didn't move, listening to him assault the door multiple times. At that rate, one of her neighbors would call the police and have him arrested.

"Go home. Please," she whispered.

"Sherry! Sherry!" The pounding became so loud and continuous that she worried he'd break down the door.

She set aside the bowl of popcorn and jumped up from the sofa. Swinging open the door, she caught Alex mid-knock, and his face reflected surprise. She caught the faint scent of gin on him, and he didn't look like himself. His bleary eyes narrowed on her. His hair was a mess and the tie on his tux askew.

"How did you get over here? Please tell me you didn't drive,"

Sherry said. She may be angry at him, but she didn't want him to do something foolish like hurt himself or anyone else.

"I didn't drive here like this. I've been drinking in the car, waiting for you. I thought you were out. I didn't know your 'plans' meant staying in." He peeped over her head. "Where is he? Is he not man enough to face me?"

He tried to come in, but Sherry pressed a hand to his chest. "Stop."

"Tell him to come face me like a man!" Alex bellowed, pounding his chest.

"Would you stop yelling?" Sherry glanced down the empty hallway. "There's no one here."

His brow furrowed. "What do you mean there's no one here? You said you had plans with someone."

"There's no one here but me. I lied, okay? I lied to keep you away, but you showed up anyway."

He cursed and swiped a tired hand down his face. "I know I shouldn't have come. I just... Forgive me. Forgive me for what I did."

She couldn't look at him. The vague ache that resided in her chest blossomed into pain at the sight of him and the tortured sound of his voice. She didn't want to hurt him but didn't know what else to do.

"I need time."

"How much?"

"I don't know."

He sighed and fell silent. Sherry continued to stare at the floor.

"I love her. She's family and I was willing to do anything to help her. What would you do for the people you love?"

Sherry lifted her teary gaze to his. "Anything."

"Then you understand."

"I do. I understand why you did it. I don't understand why you didn't tell me."

"Because I love you too, and was willing to do anything to hold on to you. It's not an excuse, *amor*. Just an explanation."

Seconds ticked by, and finally, Sherry said in a soft voice, "You can't drive in your condition."

"What do you suggest I do?"

"You can stay here," she answered. "On the couch," she added hastily.

A hint of a smile touched his beautiful face and made her ache. She missed him. Dammit, she was so weak.

Alex came forward and cupped the back of her neck. Heat splayed across her skin. Common sense told her to keep her distance, but she was starved for the feel of him and welcomed almost any contact.

She hated and loved him at the same time. Because that was what this torturous state meant—that she'd fallen in love with him and didn't know how to proceed now that she knew the whole truth.

His lips touched hers. She backed up until the doorframe dug into her spine. His other arm circled her waist and brought her flush against his body. Alex pushed his lips more firmly against hers, and she tasted the gin. Her fingers splayed out against his hard chest, and she trembled.

He moved his hips in a circular grind against hers, and for a moment she considered giving in, just throwing caution to the wind and allowing him to sweep her away with his intoxicating kiss. Fortunately, common sense prevailed.

She dragged her mouth away from his. "Don't." She kept a hand against his chest to keep from fisting his shirt and pulling him closer. Seeing him was painful enough. She couldn't afford intimacy, no matter how much her body craved him.

"I couldn't help it," he said.

"This isn't a reconciliation."

"I know, *amor*. Right now, I'll take whatever I can get."

He didn't sleep on the sofa. She let him into her bed because Alex wanted her to lay down with him. She muttered a half-hearted refusal at first, but when he looped an arm around her waist and whispered to her temple, "Don't make me beg," she caved.

They slept in the spoon position, Alex curved behind her back, his face buried in her hair and one leg thrown over her legs, as if to keep her from getting away.

It was the best sleep she'd had in a week.

❧ 14 ❧

"Hello, may I speak to Sherry Westbrook, please?"
The unfamiliar female voice on the other end of the line was rather faint.

"This is she."

"Hello, you don't know me, although you may know my name. I'm Heather, Alex's wife."

Sherry had no idea what to say. The call had completely taken her by surprise. Why would Alex's wife be calling her? She didn't need any more surprises.

"Please don't worry. I'm not calling because I'm angry or because I want to yell at you. I'm calling because I was hoping you and I could talk, for a little while, so that I could explain some things to you. Do you think it would be possible for you to come see me in the hospital?"

Sherry paced over to the window and looked out onto the street below her apartment. Her first inclination was to say no.

"Please. I won't take a lot of your time, but what I have to say to you...I think it needs to be said in person."

There was no animosity in her voice. Just a sort of pleading that broke down Sherry's wall of self-preservation. She heard herself answer, "Yes, I could come to the hospital."

"Thank you." Heather sounded relieved. "Are you available to come by today?"

"Sure."

"When?"

"Uh, I could be there in the next forty-five minutes, maybe less."

"Perfect. Thank you very much."

"Do you mind telling me what this is about? So that I can prepare for the conversation?"

"I don't want to say too much. Like I told you, it's better that we speak in person. But I wanted to explain my relationship with Alex. I promise not to keep you too long."

"All right. I'll be there."

After they hung up, Sherry second-guessed her decision. She paced the floor and wondered if she'd made a mistake. Or had Alex somehow convinced his wife to plead his case?

She shook her head. No point in trying to guess. She would simply have to go to the hospital and find out what Heather had to say.

❧

HEATHER WAS SITTING UP ON THE BED WATCHING TELEVISION WHEN Sherry arrived at the room. She stood uncertainly in the open door.

The minute she saw Sherry, Heather smiled, as if they were old friends. "Sherry?"

"Yes."

Heather waved her in. "Please, come in." She appeared to be as pleasant now as she had been on the phone. That was a good sign.

Heather's gaunt, sickly appearance reminded Sherry of the gravity of the illness that ravaged her body. She looked very much like someone knocking on death's door.

Heather turned off the television and set the remote on the

bedside table. "You can pull that chair over there next to the bed." She spoke faintly but with a warmth that made Sherry relax and believe her reservations were unfounded. She dragged the chair over to the bed and sat down.

"Thank you for coming. I wasn't sure if you would. Alex refused to give me any information about you, so I had to get your full name from Rashad, and he found your cell phone number. I hope you don't mind."

Sherry clutched the purse on her lap. "No, I don't mind."

"I have to tell you, I wasn't even sure if I should do this. It's hard to explain my relationship with Alex and Rashad. The thing is, I don't have long to live, but they both like to pretend—especially Alex—that it's not true." Pain flitted across her features, and Sherry resisted the urge to reach out and hug her. "But I know it's true." Her voice became hoarse, and she took a wavering breath, as if speaking drained her.

"Can I get you anything? Water?" Sherry asked gently.

"No, I'm fine." Heather smiled bravely. "I've known them since college. As I'm sure you know, Alex doesn't have any family to speak of. Rashad has a similar situation, and I lost both of my parents when I was very young. I grew up in foster care, and when I started college, I was on my own. It was scary at first, and then I met them, by chance. One night I went on a late food run, but I didn't have enough to cover the meal on my card. I thought I did, but I didn't, so the card declined."

She took another deep breath to bolster her strength. Sherry hung on her every word.

"Rashad was standing behind me in line, and he offered to pay for my meal. I was embarrassed, of course, but he insisted. Then he and Alex invited me to sit with them, and that's how we became friends. Three people from different walks of life, with no one else in the world, happened to find each other on a campus of almost twenty thousand students.

"We became more than friends. We became siblings, the three of us, because none of us had any. I gave them advice on women.

They gave me advice on men. We became roommates, and that only made our bond stronger, and the guys constantly looked out for me because we were family. Some people didn't understand it, but we clicked because of our similar situations. An odd ensemble of the three musketeers—the Colombian, the white chick, and the Black guy."

She smiled, and Sherry couldn't help but smile as well.

"Eventually we graduated, and they were hired into the same firm in Atlanta. I moved to Austin and worked as a contractor for a graphic design firm. It wasn't easy, but I made a living. Except I didn't have health insurance. About two years ago, I got sick, and Alex and Rashad went into protective mode."

She fell silent, plucking at the sheet with her fingers. "Alex offered to marry me, and at first I refused. I assumed that eventually I would feel better or one of the doctors would figure out what was wrong. But when I kept getting sick, he and Rashad didn't have to work as hard to talk me into it." She lifted her gaze to Sherry's. "I accepted his proposal, and we were married at the courthouse. Any expenses the insurance doesn't cover, he and Rashad take care of. They take care of me, their sister, because I have no one. They feel responsible for me, and I'm grateful, but..." She shook her head. "I no longer hold out much hope. The doctors can't fix me. I've been in and out of the hospital constantly, and this last episode has been the longest. I'm not going to make it." Her voice quivered.

"You don't know that," Sherry said.

Heather nodded. "I do. And I've made peace with it. That's why I wanted to see you, Sherry. Because of Alex, my brother." She smiled brightly. "He loves you. I understand your reservations and your concerns. But Alex and I are not your typical married couple."

"But you're still married," Sherry whispered.

"I would divorce him tomorrow if he'd let me. But his conscience won't allow it. He's afraid that if he does, I'll die. But I'm going to die anyway. He did what he could to make sure I received the care I need. He's not a bad person. So what I'm asking, Sherry, is if you could forgive him the secret he kept from you. And when I'm gone, be there for him. Because he's going to need you. And because you would make a dying woman very happy. I couldn't leave in peace knowing that I caused him to lose the love of his life."

Sherry stood. Crossing her arms, she stepped away from Heather, torn by the heartfelt words, while at the same time wondering how her conscience could handle knowing that she was involved with a married man. Even if he was married in name only.

Since he'd come to her apartment, she and Alex had been cordial to each other. They'd dined together on one occasion, but she still had her reservations and didn't go to his place or invite him to hers. She needed to keep a clear head, and spending time with him alone in either environment was too tempting a prospect.

"Sherry?"

She turned around to face Heather. The blonde's eyes were pleading and filled with tears. "He's done so much for me." Her voice quivered. "Please, let me do this one thing for him."

The tears flowed freely down her cheeks, and Sherry went to the bed and retook her seat in the chair. She took Heather's hand between both of hers.

"Please forgive him," Heather said. "I couldn't bear to know I'm the reason he can't be happy."

Sherry gently squeezed Heather's frail fingers between her own. Alex had lied to her, even knowing how important a relationship built on trust was to her. But, love was important to him. Their ideals were at odds, but his love for Heather and what he'd done to save her demonstrated his goodness. Could Sherry overlook his gross mistake?

Heather stared at her.

"I can forgive him," Sherry said.

Heather sniffed and wiped away the tears from her cheeks. A bright smile widened her face, and her dull eyes brightened a bit.

Sherry saw a hint of the vibrant young woman in the photo on Alex's bookshelf. Before the illness had stolen the brightness from her eyes, the glow in her skin, and the sheen of her hair.

"Thank you," Heather whispered. "Could you do me one more favor?"

"Of course. Anything."

"Alex said you're a praying woman. Would you pray with me?"

"Absolutely."

"Not to get better. It's too late for that."

"Anything is possible."

"Not this time. And besides, I'm ready to go. The past two years have been hell. I have one lung and can only see out of one eye. One of my kidneys has failed, I've been in a medically induced coma, and frankly, I don't have the strength I used to. I want to go in peace. Just drift away. Without pain. Would you pray with me for that?"

"I…" Sherry hesitated. People usually prayed for deliverance from illness. Not to succumb to the illness.

"I'm asking for mercy. That's all."

Sherry's bottom lip trembled as she absorbed the magnitude of the request. She clasped Sherry's hand in both of hers. "Okay. Let's pray."

⚜

ALEX OPENED THE DOOR AND STOOD IN THE DOORWAY DRESSED ONLY in a pair of sweatpants. He frowned in confusion. Ever since he'd woken up at Sherry's apartment the other day, having spent the night with her wrapped in his arms, he'd tried to respect her request for time.

"Hi," Sherry said.

"Hi."

"I went to see her."

"Who?" The frown in his brow deepened. "Heather?"

She nodded. "Rashad gave her my number." Tears filled her eyes. "I don't know what to say, except that I understand."

His chest rose and fell with a silent breath. "I should have told you about Heather right away. But everything—*we*—happened so fast."

She nodded and stared at the ground. She swallowed hard. The silence extended between them as she collected herself. Finally, she looked up into his face. "I love you," she whispered.

The words he'd been waiting to hear.

Alex spread his arms wide, and Sherry stepped into his embrace, absorbing his warmth and the familiar scent of his skin.

"I love you," she whispered again.

"I love you too, *amor*. You're all I think about. Every day. Every minute. *Solo puedo pensar en ti*." He buried his face in her neck and squeezed her tight.

Pulling her across the threshold, he kissed away her tears. They made their way to his bedroom and curled up on the bed together. He just held her, rubbing a hand up and down her spine in a soothing refrain. She wanted to get closer because she had desperately missed having this closeness with him.

"You'll wait?" he asked. "As soon as she's better, we'll get a divorce."

He was holding out hope, but Heather had already given up. Nonetheless, Sherry nodded. "Yes. I'll wait."

She held on tight, wrapping her arms and legs around him as if her life depended on it.

❧ 15 ❧

On Friday afternoon, Sherry walked up to Gina's desk. "Hi, is Alex in? I called his private line but he didn't answer. I have some papers for him to sign." She held up the documents.

"He left early. Rushed out of here a little after lunch."

"Is something wrong?"

Gina shrugged. "He didn't say, but it was definitely sudden. He told me to cancel his afternoon meetings."

"Okay. I'll get Rashad to sign off." Gnawing on her lip, Sherry walked away. Once she got Rashad's signature, she'd give Alex a call on his cell phone.

At the other end of the building, she walked up to Rashad's receptionist, a heavyset brunette with a pixie cut. "Hi, is Rashad in? I have paperwork I need him to sign."

"No. He left and didn't say when he'd be coming back. Family emergency."

Oh no. With both of them out of the office suddenly, that could only mean one thing.

Sherry went to her office, but for the next hour, she had a hard time concentrating, particularly after she tried to reach Rashad and Alex and neither one of them answered their phones. Unable to stand worrying any longer, she picked up her bag and rushed down the hall. Sailing past the receptionist at the front of the office, she called, "I'll be gone for the rest of the day."

She headed to the hospital, having no doubt that was where they were.

Sherry walked down the hall on wobbly knees. She hesitated outside Heather's room and looked through the window. Alex and Rashad were in there. Rashad sat in front of the windowsill on a chair, elbows to knees, gripping his bent head. Alex sat in a chair beside Heather's bed, holding one of her hands.

Last Saturday, Sherry had come to the hospital with Rashad and Alex. Today, Heather looked frailer than the last time Sherry had seen her, and there were extra machines in the room that hadn't been there the last time she visited, confirming the dire situation.

Sherry quietly entered the room and let the door swing closed behind her. "What happened?"

Rashad's head popped up. He directed his gaze at Alex to respond to the question. Alex glanced over his shoulder and then returned his attention to Heather.

"Her lung failed," he said in an emotionless voice. "She's on a breathing machine now. They're not holding out much hope." On the last sentence, pain, as thick as molasses, coated his voice.

Rashad winced and bowed his head into his hands again.

Sherry took one of the chairs and placed it beside Alex. He didn't look at her. He kept his attention on his friend.

Sherry took his other hand and sandwiched it between both of hers. Their fingers interlocked with each other. If nothing else, she wanted him to know that she would be there for him in his time of need.

COMPLICATIONS.

That was how the doctor explained that her heart and lung just gave up. That was why Alex, Sherry, and Rashad were standing on the deck of a boat, several miles out from the port of Savannah, with Heather's ashes in an urn.

Alex and Rashad had rented the vessel and crew from a company that conducted memorial services at sea and assisted in the scattering of ashes. Heather had always wanted to visit Savannah, and they'd promised her when she got better they would take a trip there. Just like they'd all taken a trip to Colombia, to see Alex's home. Just like they'd taken road trips back in college, scrounging up enough money to cover gas and the cost of sandwiches they made to take on their weekend adventures.

Heather never took the trip to Savannah while alive, but that didn't mean it couldn't be her final resting place. The ceremony had been short and sweet, with Alex and Rashad sharing stories about Heather to the small audience.

At the end of it, the captain said a few words and Alex handed over the urn to him. The captain crouched on the deck and, using a special device, released the ashes into the water instead of letting them float up into the air. Another crew member approached with a basket that contained red roses. All three of them—Alex, Sherry, and Rashad—selected two roses each and, one by one, tossed them into the water to float among Heather's remains.

The crew left them alone at the railing, and Sherry moved and stood between Rashad on her left and Alex on her right. Both men were stoic, jaws clenched, their expressions somber.

She took Rashad's hand and leaned her weight into Alex's arm, holding his hand tight to simultaneously receive and offer strength. In a short time, she'd fallen in love with Alex, become close to Rashad, and come to view Heather as a friend.

A tear ran unchecked down her cheek. She didn't experience the depth of pain they did at Heather's passing, but her heart still hurt that she was gone. She gained some comfort in knowing that perhaps praying with Heather over a week ago had played a small part in helping her die in peace.

But her heart hurt for Heather's two brothers, standing on either side of her, and she wished there could have been a different outcome.

❧ 16 ❧

Rain dropped to the street below and puddled on the stone terrace outside the French doors of the boutique hotel in Medellín, Colombia.

"Come back to bed." Alex's husky voice came from behind Sherry.

They'd stayed out late the night before, dancing at a small salsa bar near Parque Lleras in the upscale neighborhood of El Poblado. Afterward, they hung out in the street with the rest of the partygoers, chatting and laughing with a mix of locals and foreigners, before heading to a twenty-four-hour cafe for a quick bite and then finally returning to the hotel.

Sherry turned away from the window but left the curtains open so they could enjoy the sight of the rain as well as listen to the soothing way it hit the exterior of the building. She let Alex's shirt from the night before, which she'd pulled on as a cover-up, fall from her shoulders into a puddle on the floor.

She climbed into the bed and scooted over to Alex, and he repositioned onto his side and pulled her close. They were both naked, preferring the intimacy of sleeping skin to skin, their warm bodies in constant contact throughout the night.

Sliding a leg between both of his, Sherry groaned grumpily and pouted. "Can't we stay here forever?"

He smiled indulgently at her. "I have a business to run, and we both have clients to take care of."

"But we could work remotely, and Rashad could handle any problems that crop up in Atlanta."

"You have it all figured out, don't you?" Alex said, amused.

"I've been thinking about it, and it could work."

At least, she wanted the idea to work. Sherry had never been out of the country before, and the benefit of seeing Colombia with a native meant a more special and memorable experience. Alex knew the local hangouts and best places to visit, not just the tourist hotspots. He knew where to shop for cheap and authentic souvenirs made in-country, and the restaurants that served the best of local cuisine.

She'd tried *bandeja paisa*, often referred to as the country's national dish. Her eyes had widened when the high-calorie meal had been placed before her. The platter contained rice, fried plantains, *arepa*—a corn cake—avocado, minced meat, chorizo, black sausage, a fried pork rind, and a fried egg. Alex and the waitress had had a good laugh at her expense. She couldn't eat it all, but made such a valiant effort that she ended up stuffed and didn't eat another bite for the rest of the day.

Her favorite food discovery by far was *chocolate con queso*. At first, the idea of cheese dipped in hot chocolate did not sound appetizing, but she'd quickly grown accustomed, and it was now a breakfast staple.

"Your parents didn't even want you to come here, so they wouldn't be pleased with that arrangement," Alex pointed out. "They will accuse me of kidnapping their daughter."

"My parents gave their blessing to marry me, remember?" Sherry wiggled her hand in front of his face so he could see the marquise-cut diamond on her finger.

They'd gone to visit her parents in Kentucky at Christmas, and unbeknownst to Sherry, he'd asked for their blessing because he planned to ask for her hand in marriage while they were in Colombia. They both gave their blessing but didn't like the idea of her ringing in the New Year in Colombia. Alex had assured them Bogotá and Medellín were no less safe than any major city in the United States.

"We'll be back again, plenty of times," Alex said, rubbing a hand up and down her bare arm. "I come back at least once a year, sometimes twice. Who knows, maybe we'll buy a place here."

"Yes, let's do that. I *love* that idea."

He pulled her atop him. "And I love you." He let his hands slip below the sheet to cup her bottom.

Sherry brushed dark hair back from his forehead. "I love you too."

"*¿Cuánto?*" How much?

"*Mucho, mucho, mucho,*" Sherry whispered.

Alex cupped her face and gazed into her eyes. "*No puedo imaginarme mi vida sin ti.*"

Sherry's heart swelled with happiness. "I can't imagine my life without you, either."

She always melted when he expressed his feelings for her with such sweet words, and when he looked at her like now—all intense, his hazel eyes filled with love and speaking in his native tongue—it never failed to turn her on.

She rotated her hips against his. Never breaking eye contact, Alex squeezed her bottom and lifted his pelvis just enough to tease her with his hardening body.

"Do you have any plans for us today?" Sherry asked.

"Nothing that can't be changed," Alex replied.

Sherry threaded her fingers through the hair at his temple. "We have three days left in Medellín. How about we take a break from sightseeing and stay in to enjoy this lazy, rainy day?"

"But what will we do? How will we stay busy?" Alex frowned with faux-concern.

"Hmmm, I'm sure we can think of something."

He rolled her onto her back, and she giggled, flinging her arms around his neck.

Alex settled between her legs, heat flaring in his eyes. "I'm sure we can."

They made love, hungry kisses and firm caresses expressing their affection and desire for one another, while the thrusting motion of their hips lifted them higher to the zenith. As tension twisted in her abdomen, Sherry tightened her arms and legs around Alex, and their forged bodies rocked together in sync.

When they finally came, his guttural groans and her gasping cries mingled with the sound of rain pelting the rooftop, the exterior walls, and the windows of their temporary abode.

LOVE UNEXPECTED SERIES

To find out how Sherry's friends Shawna and Talia met their husbands and achieved their happily ever after, start the Love Unexpected series.

Fall in love with Ryan and Shawna, Tomas and Talia, Jay and Brenda, Ransom and Sophie, Diego and Ronnie, and Reed and Anika in The Blind Date, The Wrong Man, An Unexpected Attraction, The Right Time, One of the Guys, and That Time in Venice.

LATIN MEN SERIES

For more stories about Latin Men, read the entire Latin Men series with heroes from Mexico, Ecuador, Brazil, and Argentina: The Arrangement, Fight for Love, Private Acts, The Ultimate Merger, Second Chances, More Than a Mistress, and Undeniable.

ABOUT THE AUTHOR

Delaney Diamond is the USA Today Bestselling Author of sweet, sensual, passionate romance novels. Originally from the U.S. Virgin Islands, she now lives in Atlanta, Georgia. She reads romance novels, mysteries, thrillers, and a fair amount of nonfiction. When she's not busy reading or writing, she's in the kitchen trying out new recipes, dining at one of her favorite restaurants, or traveling to an interesting locale.

Enjoy free reads and the first chapter of all her novels on her website. Join her mailing list to get sneak peeks, notices of sale prices, and find out about new releases.

Join her mailing list
www.delaneydiamond.com

f facebook.com/DelaneyDiamond

🐦 twitter.com/DelaneyDiamond

📌 pinterest.com/DelaneyDiamond

CPSIA information can be obtained
at www.ICGtesting.com
Printed in the USA
LVHW041249040819
626455LV00018B/1063

9 781940 636771